CONTRACTED

AMERICA'S SECRET WARRIORS

Advance Praise for
CONTRACTED

"Operator-now-author Kerry Patton proves he's an authentic war-time novelist and gives readers a rare and true-to-life peek inside a very unique and dangerous world." **Dean Popps, former assistant secretary of the Army**

"An extraordinary tale that takes the reader inside the gray operational world of America's war against the Taliban and other Islamic extremists. America knows of its military warriors but there is another element of the struggle that goes largely unnoticed. Kerry tells the story of that group of warriors and intelligence experts in a most enjoyably readable style. You won't put this one down!" **Captain Chuck Nash, US Navy retired, military and national security commentator**

"Only through fiction can insiders tell the truth. Kerry Patton is one of the few Americans who has the perspective and experiences, both with the military and outside the wire, to write a book that mixes ground truth with an impressive story. He is an insider who is using fiction to paint truth on what has become the longest, and will soon become the most controversial war in our history." **Major Tim Lynch, US Marine Corp retired, creator of the Free Range International Blog**

"Kerry Patton brings you into the world of a warrior in the fight against radical Islam by writing a book that will impress soldier and civilian alike." **Ryan Mauro, national security analyst and author of Death to America: The Unreported Battle of Iraq**

"Kerry Patton's breakout novel, based on events the author lived, is both highly entertaining and educational. It delivers us into a world where everything is laid on the line for country and for each other. We live in a new world and with a new kind of warfare confronting America. This is a must read for those who wish to fully understand it. Highly recommended." **James Michael Pratt, *NY Times*, and *USA Today* bestselling author of *The Lost Valentine* and *Ticket Home***

"Kerry Patton's debut novel shines a light on a little-understood linchpin in 21st-century war efforts. Inspired by true events, the novel propels the reader on a journey alongside a secret fighter whose work will receive no public attention, but whose efforts are vital to national security. Patton's style adds a sense of immediacy to a finely written story." **Kay B. Day, award-winning author, and editor of *The US Report***

"Forget watching events on TV. Whether fiction or nonfiction, Kerry Patton's novel takes you to the events that impact our world and our warriors as they happen. *Contracted* is a must read for every patriot and protector of freedom. If more policy makers read this book, we'd have more solutions and less eruptions in the Middle East." **Kevin Miller, radio talk show host of *Kevin Miller in the Morning***

"Kerry Patton's novel, *Contracted: America's Secret Warriors*, confirms our deepest fears and hopes about the patriots who protect us. Like life, it raises more questions than it answers, stirs more emotions than it satisfies, and leaves us wishing we really knew the truth. I can't wait for the sequel!" **David Madeira, radio talk show host of *The David Madeira Show***

CONTRACTED

AMERICA'S SECRET WARRIORS

Kerry Patton

Quiet Owl Books

CONTRACTED

AMERICA'S SECRET WARRIORS

This book was inspired by real experiences.

To request a review copy for an article or to interview the author, please email press@quietowl.com.

Cover Design by Jennifer Welker

Published by Quiet Owl Books
quietowl.com

Quiet Owl Books are available for bulk purchases at special discounts for schools, organizations, and special events. For more information, please contact books@quietowl.com.

Read more about Kerry Patton at:
Kerry-Patton.com
QuietOwl.com/Kerry-Patton

This book is dedicated to all the men and women who gave up everything for this great nation. You shall never be forgotten.

About the Author

Kerry Patton is an internationally recognized security, terrorism, and intelligence professional. He has taught domestic and international organizations in counter-terrorism, intelligence, and physical security related issues. He has briefed some of the highest government officials ranging from ambassadors and members of Congress and Pentagon staff.

Kerry has served his country honorably throughout South America, Africa, the Middle East, Asia, and Europe, fulfilling human intelligence and physical security operations. He has conducted risk management programs on critical assets, carried out tactical surveys of more than five hundred international airfields and energy platforms, and supported in the protection of Afghan President Karzai. While operating in some of today's most classified US government programs, Kerry has interviewed (outside of interrogations) terrorists and former terrorists within multiple groups, which include Hezb Islami Gullbidine, Taliban, Maoist rebels, and the Palestinian Liberation Organization. He operated in and outside of Afghanistan from 2001 through late 2008. His knowledge of Afghanistan has been shared through numerous speaking venues from radio talk shows, academic conferences, and law enforcement seminars, to non-public government engagements.

Kerry serves as the vice president of training and public relations for the Emerald Society of the Federal Law Enforcement Agencies. He currently teaches counter-terrorism, intelligence, and protection management courses for Henley-Putnam University.

Contents

Preface

After Al Qaeda attacked the United States on the eleventh day of September in 2001, the President vowed to search for, and destroy the enemy. The United States special operations community, along with their civilian counterparts working for the CIA, was able to push Al Qaeda deep into western Pakistan and the mountainous regions of eastern Afghanistan. Although Al Qaeda was pushed, they were not defeated. With support from little-known terrorist organizations such as Lashkar-e-Taiba and Hezb Islami Khalis, Al Qaeda regrouped, re-aligned, and strengthened.

In time, US death tolls started to spike. Desperate measures were needed. In order to limit the atrocities reported on the evening news, the government used an under-spoken yet historically common tactic, and formed a unit comprised of civilians—contractors.

Many contractors were used in the open and served in multiple capacities ranging from translators and maintenance to security—many remained highly secretive in their operations.

The intelligence community has a long history of recruiting former military members as contractors for the more secretive jobs. Those wearing the uniform are often observed for years during their service. When their military service comes to an end, some become ideal operatives, later recruited by civilian government intelligence agencies to serve in covert contractual roles.

Those observing dominate the human intelligence world. They are often referred to as "talent spotters." It only took a few years after 9-11 for HUMINT'ers, as they are often called, to find and bring in a contractual force of covert operatives.

Some call these contracted warriors "guns for hire" or mercenaries. Osama bin Laden liked to refer to them as Crusaders.

American civilians were not meant to embrace the contractual force. Media would castrate their honor by disseminating propaganda about every controversy they were involved with. They would be viewed as the bad guys no matter how heroic their actions may have been. They would serve as the ultimate deception campaign, making death tolls abroad appear smaller than they really were since deaths among the contractual force would rarely be mentioned on evening news. Thousands of contractors have been killed fighting the modern Crusade started by Al Qaeda. Many more have been injured.

Few Americans know about these atrocities.

Many of these contractors had jobs in the civilian market prior to 9-11. Some were ending their own military enlistments. Many retired from the Armed Forces. Others served as first responders. A few had never picked up a gun in their lives. They all had one thing in common, and that was pure love for America. They stopped everything they were doing in their lives and rushed to the hymn of battle.

Some contractors earn more money than others. Pay ranges from tens of thousands to hundreds of thousands of dollars. At one point in America's longest war, known as the Afghan War or the War in Afghanistan, contractors were estimated to comprise more than fifty-two percent of the entire fighting force.

In this story, Declan Collins is one of those contractors. He is a former member of the US Armed Forces who later works as a contractor for the Department of Homeland Security. Declan had promised himself and his wife, Brannagh, that he would leave the military to grow a strong family. Although he separated from the service to marry his love, he remains torn because of his other passion, serving with his brothers-in-arms.

His new job working a DHS contract paid well, but it was not enough. He filled his need to connect with his military brethren by keeping up with their activities in places like Iraq and Afghanistan through news channels online.

He hated working critical infrastructure protection for DHS. Tired of the "war stories" about drug busts from the retired law enforcement officers who surrounded him in his cubicle job, Declan developed mild depression.

Very few of the men in his office had ever deployed to places like Afghanistan or Iraq. Most were clueless about the realities of fighting in a combat zone. He believed that none of his counterparts wanted to be proactive in fighting the Global War on Terror.

On one sunny autumn day, he watched a news clip of his brothers fighting abroad when he received a call that would change his life forever.

The caller asked for Declan directly and informed that his organization was looking for seasoned combat veterans. With Declan's background, he was a perfect fit for a Counterinsurgency Advisory Team in Afghanistan. When Declan asked how they found him, he was told he had been watched and referred. Declan had undergone a vast array of unique military training throughout his career, some of it classified.

Classified or unclassified, he had been watched.

The mysterious caller informed Declan he would earn three hundred thousand dollars a year and leave in two weeks. For Declan, it wasn't about money, the rush, or the desire to be a hero. It was about years of being programmed and believing in the freedoms that America's founding fathers fought and died for.

When his wife agreed to the idea of his returning to a combat zone, despite his promise, it was her support that not only made him love her more, but that pushed him to take the call to defend his country.

This story is just one picture of the contractual world made up of unconventional human intelligence operators—arguably, the world's most unsung heroes. These contractors are the people we have never heard or read about until now. Call them what you will—mercenaries, guns for hire, or Crusaders. It doesn't matter. They are patriots fighting for our freedom; they are contracted as America's secret warriors. Declan Collins is one of them and this is his story.

A Civilian's Guide to Military Abbreviations

ABP—Afghan Border Police

ACU—Army Combat Uniform

AO—Area of Operations

AOR—Area of Responsibility

ANA—Afghan National Army

ANP—Afghan National Police

ASOT—Advanced Special Operations Techniques

BDU—Battle Dress Uniform

CIA—Central Intelligence Agency

CO—Commanding Officer

CONOP—Concept of Operations

DARC—Direct Action Resource Center

DC—Deputy Commander

DFAC—Dining Facility

DOD—Department of Defense

DHS—Department of Homeland Security

FOB—Forward Operating Base

FOBBIT—Slang acronym for Forward Operating Base Hobbit

FRAGO—Fragmentation Order

GPS—Global Positioning System

HMMWV—High Mobility Multipurpose Wheeled Vehicle (pronounced "Humvee")

HUMINT—Human Intelligence

HUMRO—Humanitarian Relief Operations

HVT—High-Value Target

IC—Intelligence Community

IED—Improvised Explosive Device

INSCOM—Intelligence and Security Command

JSOC—Joint Special Operations Command

KIA—Killed in Action

LZ—Landing Zone

MACV—Military Assistance Command Vietnam

MEDVAC—Medical Evacuation

MRAP—Mine Resistant Ambush Protected Vehicle

NGO—Non-Government Organization

NVG—Night Vision Goggles

ODA—US Special Forces Operational Detachment Alpha (A Team), Direct Action Team

ODB—US Special Forces Operational Detachment Bravo (B Team), Support Team

OGA—Other Government Agency

OPORD—Operations Order

POLAD—Political Advisor

POTUS—President of the United States

PRT—Provincial Reconstruction Team

PSYOP—Psychological Operations

SATCOM—Satellite Communications

SBS—Special Boat Service (United Kingdom)

SECDEF—Secretary of Defense

SERE—Survive, Evade, Resist, Escape

SF—Special Forces

SIGINT—Signals Intelligence

SOF—Special Operations Force

S2—Military Intelligence Officer

TACP—Tactical Air Control Party

TOC—Tactical Operations Center

UAV—Unmanned Aerial Vehicles

VBIED—Vehicle Born Improvised Explosive Device

WIA—Wounded in Action

Prologue

Declan Collins sat in his hotel room watching the evening news. Tomorrow would be the start of a long journey. A communiqué from an Al Qaeda leader aired on nationally syndicated media outlets. Declan's body filled with excitement. The person he watched, the person who called American citizens infidels and our military members Crusaders, would soon be hunted. Declan, set to leave for Afghanistan tomorrow, embraced the call to battle.

A subtle knock on the hotel door drew him up. Declan knew who it was. The person behind the door was a stranger who would soon become a brother—it was Rex Bowbart, Declan's new team leader.

"You ready?" the physically fit, balding team leader asked as Declan opened the door.

"Just finishing up this letter."

Declan had dressed for the occasion. The two were about to go out and eat one last meal at a decent restaurant. It would be several months before they encountered such luxuries as a finely cooked meal.

"I hope you don't plan on giving me that letter." Rex knew exactly what it was: a "party foul" letter.

"Sorry, Rex." Declan glanced at the paper he held in his hand before placing a few hundred dollar bills and the letter in an envelope. "You know what to do with this."

"Yeah, I know what to do with it." Rex snatched Declan's letter from his hand.

The money enclosed would be used to buy drinks for everyone who showed up at his funeral should one be needed. In the operator world, if you missed your last "hoorah," you committed a party foul.

"Considering it's just you and me on this operation, I figured I had no one else to trust with mine either. So here. Don't lose it."

Declan knew Rex's letter would probably go back and forth between past and present tense too. Written by operators to say their last goodbyes, these letters were written as though the dead were speaking to those still alive.

"Hopefully no one will ever need to read these." Declan put on his leather jacket and the two walked out the door.

✝✝✝

I did a job you all know I was overly proud of. Many of you never knew what I was doing or who I was working for, but don't feel bad. Most of the time I didn't know the answer to these questions. That's the life of a contractor. Either way, I believed in this country to the point that I was willing to die for it. Many people say that the dream of a fisherman is to die at sea with his ship; well, I too would never have wanted to go any other way than how I did: serving my country.

Many times Bin Laden himself called people like me Crusaders. I took this as a compliment. A Crusader was someone willing to leave their loved ones, who were strong enough to support this commitment, to go fight for the oppressed in the name of God. While many of you may not realize this, that's exactly what I was doing. I loved every second of it.

Our currency states, "In God We Trust." I trust in my God, my country, and my family. You all played a part in molding me into the person I once was. Do not be angered by our country's leadership because of my death.

3

Thank our leadership for not giving up on this fight, and thank them for ensuring that each and every one of you remains free today. Men like me and my brothers, who I loved, serving alongside, are happy and willing to selflessly fulfill the ultimate sacrifice. With that said, stop your damn crying!

Mom and Dad, a guy like me could never have dreamed of better parents than you. You taught me to never quit no matter how hard it gets. Never settle for average; average is easy. Beyond average is difficult but the reward for the work is incredible. You taught me to fight for what I believed in. Most importantly, you taught me how to love.

Brannagh ~ Love is so wonderful. I've never loved you more than when you agreed to let me go. Thank you for trusting me, time and again. I know you understand that the only reason I would face this kind of danger is for you and our country.

Brannagh, you are beautiful, so stop feeling sorry for yourself and wipe those tears away!

I'm sorry I couldn't give you the baby you always wanted.

You have a whole bunch of kids already, though. Being a teacher, you have one of the most rewarding jobs. Each one of your students is your child. I see your passion and how you love those kids in a way that only a mother could.

I know you will never go to bed without giving Apoc a hug and kiss for me. I mean, c'mon, you give him a million a day. But if the day is tough and he is ticking you off, please don't let that stop you from letting that ninety-five-pound shedding beast of an American bulldog from knowing his Daddy loved him.

Ardan and Marie, thank you for allowing me to be a part of your lives. Thank you for allowing me to marry Bran.

You all have taught me so much. I wish you all the best, and please never forget those that served. I know you won't. I love you all.

To end this, way too long, dragged out, virtually impossible thing to write, I can't stress this enough—I love all of you! I did what I believed in, and I promise, I will always be looking down on you, so whenever you want to chat, let me know: I am forever by your side.

Look, I haven't even left for overseas yet and I am crushed with tears, so enough is enough. I need to stop feeling sorry for myself. I love you all! God Bless and feel a huge warm kiss and hug.

No Regrets!
Declan Collins

PART I

ONE

A n explosion ripped the air. The noise of flying metal momentarily deafened Declan Collins. A blinding white light pierced the early evening darkness. He froze, dazed, as the blast penetrated the perimeter wall close to where he had been standing just moments before. Shocked, he forced himself to maintain his situational awareness. If he lost that, he knew, he'd lose everything.

Many expletives ran through his head, but Declan was trained for times like these. Without thinking, he was capable of channeling his emotions, ensuring that he remained focused.

Find some cover.

Lower your heart rate.

Control your breathing.

"C'mon," his team leader, Rex Bowbart, shouted as he ran toward the interior of the safe house. "We're under attack!"

Non-government organization workers flooded the infamous Haj safe house every Thursday night. It was the first evening the two military advisors had set foot inside the tucked-away watering hole.

Few knew the Haj was operated through US government funds. They were secret funds, coming out of a unique Office of the Director of National Intelligence program. On the surface, the Haj was used to help Afghan students learn computer skills, which included use of the Internet. Behind the scenes and during the evening hours when the Afghans weren't around, it was used as a collaboration mechanism for non-government organizations to discuss activity in the regions they operated. It was a true honeypot for intelligence. But even the NGOs coming in and out didn't know the whole truth behind the Haj—excluding Baba Rich.

Declan took cover opposite the initial impact area. "That was probably just a small VBIED," he said. "So much for Dr. James saying this place is safe."

"I get the impression that no one here comprehends that word." Rex pulled out his till-then concealed 9mm from behind his back, ready to kill any Afghan insurgent storming the house. "A vehicle born IED just detonated right outside this place and some think it's still safe because a few local Afghans were hired to secure the perimeter and entry point. You've got to be kidding me."

With his pale skin and linebacker build, Rex looked like a Viking warrior. His curly blond hair failed to cover a growing bald spot, etched by years of war. Hair loss wasn't the worst price to pay. Seeing this guy who was ten years his senior, and still so physically and mentally fit, filled Declan with awe.

"Over here," Baba Rich, the American expat living at the Haj, shouted. "It's all clear."

"Isn't that the former Marine colonel yelling at us?" Declan asked Rex as he tried to get the ringing out of his ears.

"Yeah." Rex headed toward Baba Rich. "Let's go. Stay down."

Declan hurried, maintaining a low silhouette as he followed his team leader. The three of them took positions near the rear door of the safe house, maintaining a good line of sight on the partially destroyed perimeter wall of the compound.

Several minutes passed. Declan could hear no gunshots. *Good.* That meant this was a single incident and not a complex attack. Surely a few

9mms and Baba Rich's AK-47 would be no match for an enemy assault team storming the place.

"Welcome to Afghanistan, gents." Baba Rich looked through the crumbling perimeter wall. "That was one hell of an explosion."

"VBIED?" Declan asked, taking in the man's appearance.

His elongated face covered with a salt-and-pepper beard made him look more Pashtun than the Scotch-Irish American he was. His elderly, war-seasoned facial structure made Baba look fatherly to the younger NGOs coming in and out of the Haj. This is how he assumed the name Baba—meaning father. He was a fatherly figure, a protector.

"Brother, if that was a VBIED, you wouldn't be here right now." Baba continued searching for any additional threat in the area. "That wasn't a VBIED. No, that was one heck of a regular, old, improvised explosive device placed somewhere on the street. You're lucky."

"Tell me about it." Declan wiped dust off his face.

"Dude, you flew like ten feet backwards. You must have nine lives," Baba added.

"Two weeks into this hell hole, and you already made it through a bomb blast." Rex clapped Declan on the back.

"How many months of this crap do I have to deal with?"

"C'mon, your first explosion deserves a celebration." Baba Rich moved to the safe house's poolside tiki bar. "Rum and coke anyone?"

Declan believed his new friend, Baba, was either insane or a genius. Who in his right mind would start serving up drinks immediately after an attack? To Baba Rich, Declan thought, the incident had to be treated as just part of another day in paradise.

Twelve NGOs appeared from the safe house's interior and headed toward the bar. Chim-Chim, who worked for Baba Rich, inspected the blast site. He was a short tech-geek kid and an MIT grad. His light brown beatnik beard was so long, it looked as if he were growing it for a contest.

An academic innocent, Chim-Chim saw only the need to bring peace and harmony into Afghanistan. Declan accepted him for who he was, a man trying to do good yet failing to see the tactical complexities of war.

The rum and coke was warm and potent. It burned all the way down. Declan downed another good-sized swallow.

"Well?" he asked.

"Doesn't look like it was intended for us," Chim-Chim said after inspecting the damage. "Seems like they were targeting the school across the street."

"Who the hell would ever put a safe house near a school?" Rex asked.

"The Aussies." Baba Rich continued to play bartender. "They were here long before we were. Hell, they built the place. We took it over once they left."

"Think it's time to move?" Declan asked.

"Nope," Baba Rich said. "See these guards? Every one of them was either Taliban or has family who was Taliban."

"You gotta be kidding me," Rex blurted. "Taliban?"

"Let me explain something to you two." Baba Rich took a seat behind the bar. His dark skin had the texture of leather. "There are two types of Taliban—the Afghan Taliban and the Pakistani Taliban. Worry about the Pakistanis. The Afghans, you can work with them as long as you're respectful and have money."

"But they're Taliban," Declan said.

"Most Afghan Taliban became that out of fear." He lit a cigarette, and the silver in his beard glinted in the bright moonlight. "Forced into it, if you will. Some needed the money. Our guys, they needed the money, so now that we can pay them, they're the best security in the entire region. Awesome intel sources too."

"And they are actually willing to share intel with you?" Declan placed his glass on the bar. He needed to pace himself.

"Sure. They tell the best stories, and when you decipher what they're saying, they reveal a lot of ground truth."

"Yeah," Rex said, "but how reliable is their information?"

"It's better than anything the military has." Baba Rich pointed his cigarette at one of the guards. "See that one over there? His dad, Mehsud Haq, is a famous warlord here in Nangarhar. Has his own militia. Good guy to be friends with, which is why Haji Haq is my number-one guy. Anywhere I go, he comes with me. People fear him and his dad."

"That's Haji Haq?" Declan exclaimed.

Rex took out a small notepad and paper. "When we come back next Thursday, is there any way Declan and I can stick around? Kind of hang out with you for a couple days?"

"I don't see why not. We got plenty of space here."

"Here, this is my Roshan cell number." Rex handed over the piece of paper. "Do me a favor and give me a call tomorrow."

"No problem." Baba Rich took a set of car keys out of his pocket. "I'll do one better, though. I have to go over there tomorrow to pick up some mail. Was gonna get a workout in too. Let's link up for dinner. I'm tired of eating Afghan food every day."

"Sounds like a plan."

Declan was hesitant to say anything.

There was no way Colonel Davis, the Brigade deputy commander, would allow Rex and him to stay off base. But then, he didn't believe half of what he had seen so far in Afghanistan.

✝✝✝

"Do you really think this is going to happen?" he asked Rex as they made it back to their designated Forward Operating Base late that evening. "If the colonel found out that we were off tonight without any military escort, he'd likely confine us to base, or worse, kick us out of country."

"He didn't know we could sneak off base tonight." Rex opened his laptop. "Don't you worry about Colonel Davis. He likes me already since I'm an LSU football fan, and he's for Ohio State."

"Hey, I'm game if you pull this off." Declan lay down on his cot. "I just don't want to piss anyone off too soon."

"Shhh." Rex propped himself up.

Sporadic cracking filled the air.

"Yeah, I heard it too," Declan said.

"It sounds like it's east of us. Gunfire. It's coming from the perimeter of the base."

"I guess I'll be sleeping with my gun tonight." Declan turned off his headlamp.

As exhausted as the day and the rum had left him, he knew there was no way he'd sleep well knowing the base could be overrun during the night. For the first time, he realized the kind of danger he was in. He wasn't just part of the brotherhood anymore. He was risking his life for it.

TWO

D eclan fell asleep playing out various scenarios for the night, all of them brutal. The thought of being captured and displayed, beheaded, on YouTube was his greatest fear. He didn't want to be another Nick Berg. He wanted to finish this job unscathed, and he wanted to be back home again with Bran, his newlywed wife. He had signed on to this contract knowing he would make good money and again embrace the sense of true patriotism he once had while wearing a military uniform. All the while, he would endure an adventure that far surpassed anything many could fathom. But the adventure was turning out to be more frightening than he had bargained for.

The early morning Afghan sun shone brightly on him as he walked out of his sleeping quarters. He had awakened desperately wanting to make one quick phone call. A hundred minutes had been added to his Roshan cell phone. He kept two cells on him at all times. One was for general use. The other he used for one reason only, and that was to make contact with Spartacus, the man who had recruited him five years earlier and the only one he trusted.

A seasoned, American covert operative, Spartacus had been in the CIA for more than twenty-seven years. Close to sixty years of age, he was positioned by the government in southeastern Maryland, where he operated from his home close to the Naval Academy. The chiseled, muscular man had thick white hair and a matching moustache and could compete in a powerlifting competition. And he was more than a handler.

He was a father figure who had taught Declan a lot about life, even beyond their work together.

Spartacus had provided Declan with specific directives prior to his entering Afghanistan. *Only make contact when the game changes. Never forget that you're simply a military advisor. And last, don't reveal to anyone that I exist.* After the previous night's explosion, the game had changed.

He made the call where he would attract the least attention— across the tarmac in his wooden B-Hut office. A small team of Army troops ran past in their PT uniforms, wearing reflective belts. He admired their dedication. Not just the dedication to staying in shape, but the commitment to staying fit in order to take the fight to the enemy. Whether he knew them or not, they were his brothers, and he felt an urge to support them any way he could. They were his reason for being in Afghanistan.

"It's Declan."

"How you making out?" The military-deep voice of his one and only true friend came on the line.

"Everything's fine," he said. "You told me to call when things changed. Well, a game changer is already in the works."

"Talk to me."

"We met some NGOs. Rex and I believe they're worth getting close to." Declan switched the phone to his left ear. The constant ringing in his right made it difficult to hear. "We're working a new system, going to try and stay with them for a little while."

"You think you guys can pull this off?"

"Rex does. He's confident." He ducked from a plume of dust headed in his direction. "We'll have to stay off base at a safe house. That's the sketchy part. Last night, an IED went off right next door, targeting a nearby school. Caused some damage to the perimeter wall, but the housekeeper swears up and down that the place is safe."

"Remember lesson number one, which I taught you long ago," Spartacus said like the professional he was. "You have to assess whether the risk is worth the reward."

The man had a point. Images flashed through Declan's head. The sounds and sights of the night before. Previous interactions with the brigade he supported, and some good times spent with Bran. If anything happened, he knew she would understand. In his mind, the risk was definitely worth the reward.

"The place is one large system filled with multiple networks." Declan made it to his office door. "Too many potential assets and sources not to try this. It's an intelligence honeypot that no one has tapped yet."

"How long are you guys shooting for?"

"Initially, one week." Declan watched a herd of local Afghan workers pass by him and head off to build some hardened sleeping quarters on the base. "We'll report back to the DC in one week. Hopefully he'll see the value in having us off the yard. If everything goes as planned, we'll try making it our new home."

"Who's the deputy commander over there?"

"A guy by the name of Colonel Davis. He's a real warmonger. Someone you'd like. Believes being the DC is better than being the ultimate boss." The office's air conditioner clicked on automatically and Declan walked a few paces away from it. "The guy likes my buddy Rex a lot. He doesn't seem to be the traditional commander type, wanting to do everything by the book. A real rule-bender, if you will. His boss takes all the flack when things go astray. The DC has some good protection with the full bird."

"Wait a minute." Spartacus paused. "You guys have a full bird as the DC and a full bird as the CO?"

"Davis just tacked it on. After this tour, he takes over Ranger training as the CO down in Fort Benning."

Declan spotted Rex and another operator heading in his direction. His time was running out.

"Listen, I gotta run. Company's coming."

"E-mail me letting me know you guys have the green light to go outside the wire without an escort from the DC. Send me the coordinates of the site as well."

"Roger that. If we do this, just so you know, I'll be off the radar for a while." Declan waved at Rex, who was only yards away.

"Got it. Try keeping me in the loop at least once a week."

"Roger that."

With Spartacus fully aware of what was happening, Declan felt an ounce of security. He knew that his mentor's ability to assist would be limited if the mission went astray, but him having the coordinates of the Haj could expedite some type of rescue if it came to that. At a minimum, the coordinates would provide a foundation for good intel regarding Declan's last-known location. He appreciated every bit of added security and could only hope it was enough.

THREE

Computers sat on improvised wooden desks. An air conditioner droned on. Different colored thumbtacks cluttered the maps posted around the walls, and most important, one still-operable coffee pot brewed the caffeine necessary for them to make it through the day. Declan hated his coffin-like office. His passion was being out in the field, speaking with locals, gathering intelligence, and learning the ins-and-outs of Afghanistan. He grabbed some paper cups and wondered how anyone could be happy spending eight to twelve months on that base.

"Sorry, sir, we didn't get any creamer yet from the DFAC," he explained to Captain Jack. "We have plenty of sugar, though."

"Please, call me Jack." The Navy O-6 took the cup of freshly made hot joe from Declan. "I'm surprised you were even able to grab sugar from the chow hall."

"My friend, that's what we're good at," Rex chimed in. "We don't steal. We procure."

Declan soon realized that Rex and Jack had a past. The two obviously knew one another from a former life. Finding out what that common ground was would determine the value of the Navy officer. As Spartacus had taught him, everyone had some type of value, but to what degree made all the difference in the world.

"So I take it you two know each other?" he asked and passed a cup over to Rex.

"Met at DARC about three years ago," Rex said. "Thanks for the joe, *mi amigo*."

"We had a blast there," Captain Jack added. "Direct Action Resource Center. Now that's where you learn some tricks of the trade."

"I love that place," Rex said.

Bingo! Captain Jack wasn't just some military drone. No, he was a high-ranking officer who was in this for the long haul. No one went to DARC just for the fun of it. People chose that training center because they took their jobs seriously. Only the best of the best attended DARC training in Arkansas. If you wanted advanced firearms, advanced tactics, advanced anything pertaining to military or law enforcement, you went to DARC and embraced training conducted by former Delta and special operators. Captain Jack was the real thing.

"Jack here, well, he's with a small, unique team of JSOC-PSYOP folks." Rex sat behind his desk, checking some e-mails as he spoke. "Correct me if I'm out of line here, Brother Jack, but would you agree that we could probably do more good for your guys than for Brigade?"

"Absolutely."

Declan swung his chair around. "Rex, seriously, do you really believe Brigade will just let us do whatever we want?"

"Little Brother," Rex replied with a grin, "you watch and learn how I get things done around here."

Captain Jack began to laugh. "I guess you two don't know one another all that well."

"Well enough to know I wouldn't want to operate alongside anyone else," Rex said. "Mr. Collins, Jack here is an O-6 with JSOC. He reports directly back to higher headquarters, and he's our ticket to receiving the keys to the kingdom."

Clearly his team leader was on a similar brain wave as he. The two needed every human asset with any amount of pull. Jack was definitely one of those people.

"What's the catch?" Declan asked.

"No catch," Captain Jack replied. "You guys have capabilities my team and I just don't have. We need you, and well, it seems like from what Rex told me earlier at breakfast, you guys need us."

"Do you have the power to get us to walk the thin red line here? That fine line that borders breaking the rules, Captain?" Declan began to drink his coffee.

"I have only the tools." Jack rested his elbows on his knees and placed both hands under his chin.

"He can get us access to the different compounds, introduce us to some folks we'll need to become friends with. You know, those keys to the kingdom," Rex explained. "If we stay within the confines of Brigade, we won't do a thing for the next several months."

"Do you guys really want to be stuck on base throughout your entire deployment?" Jack asked.

"I get it." Declan stood up. "Rex, you want to do all this stuff, but we haven't even sighted in our weapons since we stepped foot here. There's still a lot we have to do before we go fully operational." Declan looked at Captain Jack.

"You want to sight in your weapons?" he asked, and began tying his bootlaces. "Too easy. Come over to my compound, and we'll get you access badges made up. You can come and go as you please. Shoot all the rounds you want. Eat at our chow hall, swim in our pool. Anything you need."

"That easy?" Declan asked.

"That easy."

"Rex, don't you have a meeting with the DC?" Jack asked as he walked toward the door.

"Damn. Almost forgot." He jumped to his feet. "You ready, Declan? We gotta go."

"I'll swing back here in a couple of hours." Captain Jack paused at the door. "Good luck with your meeting. Oh yeah, before I forget, Declan, can you accompany one of my guys around 1700 this evening? He's hosting a meeting with some tribal elders from across the border."

"Yeah, no problem."

As Jack left the room, Declan was sure this Navy buddy of Rex's would come in handy. He had access to things Declan would probably need. Being able to borrow weapons, weapons like AKs used by the locals, was good enough, but Jack's rank and position were the icing on the cake.

"That guy's the shizzle." Rex opened the door and headed out to see Colonel Davis.

"Yeah." Declan followed him. "He may very well be our saving grace here."

"At least one of 'em," Rex agreed.

Colonel Davis's office was almost in sight. *Be patient, don't say a lot, observe, and play the game.* That's what he needed to do.

FOUR

Passing the frenzied activity inside the tactical operations center, Declan was disappointed yet amused at the number of troops in uniform sitting around doing a lot of nothing.

His thoughts evaporated once he saw the frumpy, silver-haired colonel joking with his operations officer. Declan knew Rex was about to request something big. It was time to get serious.

"Ah, my two favorite civilians," Colonel Davis greeted them. "What can I do you for?" Everyone was his favorite. Declan knew this was just his way of appearing upbeat.

"Well, LSU will make it to the BCS Championship game while Ohio State eats popcorn watching a game they won't even be in this year." Rex broke the ice but was careful not to give anything away.

"Would you believe this guy?" The colonel pointed at Rex. "How do you put up with him?"

"It's not easy, sir."

"Well, look at what I just found." The colonel reached for an Ohio State baseball cap. "Speak to me while I wear this the whole time."

"Let's go." Rex looked to Declan as he gestured to the door. He turned back to Colonel Davis. "I can't bear being in the same room with you while you wear that thing."

"You can't just leave. I'm your boss." Davis took off his alma mater's hat. "Is this better? Geez, I can't even kid around with you, Dr. Rex."

"Oh, of course you can. But not until your team wins another BCS."

Colonel Davis laughed. "Take a seat."

Seeing the two of them interact was like watching a sitcom, yet Declan knew that beneath the kidding was a mission that was deadly serious. If things went as planned, Colonel Davis could be another key asset, as long as he was willing to turn a blind eye every once in a while.

"Colonel, I know your guys don't really care for advisors like us," Rex said and stroked his beard. "Well, I think I have a solution that will keep us out of your hair yet still be valuable."

"Who said we don't like you guys? I love you two." Colonel Davis snickered. "OK, you're right. Most of us uniforms can't stand folks like you."

"And we know this, which is why we're here."

"What? Did my first sergeant hurt your feelings or something?"

"No, sir." Rex flexed his linebacker biceps. "You really think that twerp has anything on these guns?"

"You gotta love this guy." Colonel Davis shook his head, but Declan knew he was waiting for them to divulge why they'd come.

"So here's the skinny." Rex's tone was matter-of-fact. "We need a favor."

Here it comes, Declan thought. *Please, Colonel, don't drop the denial bomb.*

"What kind of favor?"

"Declan and I need to disappear for a couple of days."

"And where do you two think you're going?"

"Let's just say that if you called either one of us on our Roshans and needed us, we would be available within a half-hour."

"I don't want to ask anything else, do I?" The colonel had finally realized that Rex was serious.

"Probably not, sir."

Declan was dumbfounded. Rex was about to pull off the impossible. If any other Colonel heard this request, he knew it would absolutely be shot down.

"OK, I'm good with your crazy ass disappearing for a couple of days." He glanced at Declan. "Should I assume that you're willing to play this madman's game as well?"

"Yes, sir." Declan tried to hide his surprise.

"One condition, men."

Declan braced himself. *Please, no convoy nonsense, no extra bodies. God what is about to come out of this man's mouth?*

"You can't take off until after tonight's huddle meeting, and you must be back here by next Friday's huddle."

Declan, who had attended two, hated the weekly meetings where military leaders from Brigade, Special Forces, JSOC, and the advisors came together to discuss current and future operations. He knew Rex hated them even more. They both believed the huddles were a waste of time, especially when high-value targets were briefed, yet no one had physical descriptions of the terrorists. The best they had were silhouettes, which they showed on PowerPoint slides. Declan hoped that being off base for a while could change that.

"Next Friday it is, sir." Rex got up and headed for the door.

"Mr. Collins," the colonel barked. "Keep an eye out for your little partner here."

"Who you calling little?" Rex grinned and flexed his muscles.

"C'mon." Declan began pulling his team leader out of the office. "I'll make sure he comes home to his Daddy in one piece, sir."

"Yeah, you hear that, Dr. Rex?" Davis put his Ohio State hat back on as they made their way to the door. "I'm your Daddy."

"Thanks, Colonel." Declan waved. "We'll see you in a week."

Sudden relief surged through him. Colonel Davis was either a mad man, who couldn't care less about rules, or he simply didn't care what happened to his two military advisors. But that wasn't the point. All that mattered was that he and Rex had just been given the green light to do something outside the wire that very few would know anything about. He couldn't wait to get started.

FIVE

E ager to begin the unique operation, Declan needed to do one last thing prior to heading out. A group of Pakistani tribal leaders from the Mohmand Tribe was to gather at a nearby Provincial Reconstruction Team base with one of Captain Jack's team members.

He had no issue with going. He was confident that it would be short and to the point. Until he walked into the meeting room. He'd been forewarned that a political advisor from the US State Department may attend. And sure enough, Travis Shiller, the ever-detested political advisor, was present. He could wait.

Declan spotted Jack's man easily. He wore trekking boots, tan cargo pants, and a tan T-shirt that exposed a mild bulge in his mid-section. His beard was sandy brown and as thick as his hair.

Declan approached him. "You must be one of Jack's guys."

"Was told you would be here. Declan, right? Call me Shrek."

Their introduction was short-lived. Travis Shiller, a six-foot-five, three-hundred-pound sloth with a reputation for pomposity, jumped in.

"I don't have a sexy call sign like you guys," he said in a hollow voice. "I'm Travis."

The second Declan shook his hand he knew to be cautious. He felt a negative vibe right from the get-go. Shrek obviously felt it too, as he was quick to take his seat.

A flock of Pakistani tribal elders entered the room. As they sat down, silence filled the air. No one was willing to take the lead in the conversation, so Declan greeted them and began his rapport building.

Shrek pulled out a notepad and began scribbling. Travis sat and observed. Time was limited. The visitors needed to travel back across the border soon, and Declan had to show up at the evening's huddle meeting.

Minutes passed, and a lot of small talk ensued. Passive questioning wouldn't work. He needed to find out why the Pakistanis had requested the meeting. Declan needed to be direct. "We want to help you. We want to help the Pashtun people. Tell me what the Pashtun people need from us."

He wasn't prepared for their answer. No one was. The leader of the Pakistanis stood and announced, "We need weapons."

"Weapons?" Travis bellowed and perched in his seat, alarmed.

The jerk had failed to initiate the conversation; therefore, he needed to resume as a fly on the wall. Declan glanced over at him, giving him a silent warning to stand down. Travis complied.

"Do you believe the Pakistani government will not protect you?" Declan played dumb; he knew the government was just as corrupt as the Taliban. "Why do you need weapons? I thought everyone in the tribal regions had their own."

"We can no longer protect ourselves," said the skinny, gray-bearded elder of the group who had introduced himself as Hukam. "Taliban comes in and steals our children. They rape our women. When the government comes, they do the same."

"So why don't you rise up and fight them?" Declan asked and leaned forward in his chair.

Hukam stood and pointed at Travis in disgust. "Your State Department took our guns away from us."

"If we can get your weapons back, will you fight the Taliban and join with the United States?" Declan asked in a calm voice.

The tribesmen appeared pleased. He could see their expressions transform from concern to admiration. Then he looked over to Shrek, hoping this was the change he wanted to see. Shrek nodded.

In the background, the daily call to prayer at evening could be heard, but Declan kept the lead. "The Mohmand people are an honorable people," he said. "You have a history of being fierce warriors. Will you join with us and help destroy the Taliban if we get you weapons?"

As if it were a pep rally, the elders became boisterous, praising Declan's willingness to assist them. They didn't care about making it to evening prayer. The fire was stoked. Declan had them exactly where he needed them.

Travis stood, and the mood in the room quickly changed. His round cheeks were bright red, and the emotions behind the fake smile were clear.

"Gentlemen, thank you for coming this evening." Travis rushed himself over to the Pakistanis and began ushering them out of the room. "We don't want you to miss prayer."

As Travis walked the elders out of the room, Shrek and Declan looked at one another, and Declan could see that his new friend was as confused as he was. Shrek closed his notepad and stashed his pen into his pant cargo pocket.

"I thought this was your show," Declan told him, then adjusted his concealed 9mm behind his back.

"It is my show." Shrek walked closer to the door to listen for any outside conversation. "Here he comes. I can hear him breathing."

The door flew open. It slammed into the wall and left a hole in the plaster. The beet-red face of Travis glowed with anger. The rolls of fat under his arms swayed as he pointed at Declan.

"Who are you? Who the hell do you work for?" he shouted and crossed the room toward Declan.

Travis must have realized that the much smaller operator wasn't going to be bullied by some out-of-shape behemoth. Good thing because Declan had just about reached the end of his patience. "Just tell me who you work for."

"Travis, you know who I work for. I'm a military advisor." Declan didn't let his guard down. "I was asked to come here by Shrek's boss. I came and did what was asked. Now, what is your issue with that?"

"You were asked to get these guys weapons?" His voice rose.

His former life working law enforcement had taught Declan how to respond. As long as Shrek was his witness, he knew how to play the game.

"Travis, I promise you, if you speak to me like that again, or take another step toward me, I will defend myself against a perceived threat."

"What? You're going to beat me up?" He walked closer, high on his own perceived power.

Declan took one step back and raised his left hand. With his right, he grabbed the pistol from behind his back, leaving it holstered but prepared to be shot if needed. "No, you stupid shit. I will kill you."

Shrek jumped between the two of them and faced Travis. "Hey, man, this was my show," he said. "You were invited here only because Brigade's POLAD asked to have you present. We have a good relationship with him. You were supposed to sit here and simply observe. You didn't like what you heard and ruined everything, not having a clue what the hell we were doing."

"Oh, I know what you were doing all right. You were about to give guns away to locals!"

"No, stupid, we were going to provide inert weapons with tracking devices imbedded in them." Shrek stepped aside and looked at Declan. "Dec here was our mediator. He did exactly what we wanted him to do."

"None of this falls within our strategy." Travis refused to admit his error. "This is not what we are here to do."

"Show me a written, multi-organizational strategy for Afghanistan, Travis." Declan felt his ears grow warm. "There hasn't been a written strategy since Under SECDEF Doug Feith wrote one in 2001."

Travis stood silent. Declan refused to let the situation go. "Your organization came into country thinking it could change everything with this peace, love, and happiness bullshit, and you run things as if you're all on the same page. Let me tell you something. No one here knows what the hell the strategy is anymore."

"But…"

"But nothing. The only strategy I live by is to do whatever is needed to keep our guys alive. And if that means we need to start wars between the tribes, then so frickin' be it."

Declan took a deep breath and looked at the clock mounted on the wall. It was getting late. He had made his point and was now wasting his time with the State Department. "I have to be at a meeting."

"Wait up. I'm coming with you." Shrek grabbed his things and followed Declan out of the room.

"I'm writing a report about this," Travis shouted as he stood alone in the empty room.

"Screw you and your stupid ass report, Travis," Declan called back and continued his walk to the huddle brief.

"You know his reports go straight up to the National Security Council?" Shrek turned on his headlamp, ensuring he could see as he walked through the early-evening Afghan darkness.

"Good. Let him make me famous back at the Beltway." Declan tried to put the incident behind him.

No luck. He was livid. Such blunders happened too frequently lately. No one was operating on the same page. Conventional Army did their thing while Special Forces did something else. State and DOD never proved capable of working together. Contractors were hated by everyone.

Declan didn't care about any of that. He only cared that the guys operating were safe. He cared about his brothers, and he cared about returning to Bran in one piece. There was no time to think about that right now, though. Shrek and he were already late for the huddle.

SIX

To Declan, the huddle resembled King Arthur and the *Knights of the Round Table*. Army officers listened to the briefing intently while a handful of bearded Special Forces members yawned. The room was mentally split. Declan didn't find the briefing nearly as interesting as he did the observations of those sitting in the room.

Meeting adjourned. Griff, the Special Forces S2, walked out with his boss, Hooch, who wore woodland BDUs. That meant Special Forces. The conventional army wore ACUs, which were gray and checkered instead of the mottled gray, green, and black. Neither man appeared impressed by what he had just heard. Declan and Rex followed them out the door into the cold Afghan night.

They walked far enough to separate themselves from the herd that had stayed behind, smoking and joking.

Declan could not resist. He felt the need to probe the two Special Forces operatives to find where they stood after enduring the huddle.

"I will never get those two hours of my life back," he said.

Griff, who was walking in front of him, turned around with a grin. Tall and heavy-set, he had round rosy cheeks that, before he said a word, revealed his easygoing nature.

"Was that a waste of time or what?" Declan said. Having Captain Jack and Colonel Davis support them was a start. Adding some spec ops guys into the mix could make for the perfect concoction. "You guys have to sit through that every Friday evening?"

"Not if I have anything to do with it." Griff's short, stout companion grinned through his black beard. "I'm Hooch. This is my intel guru, Griff."

"Third Group?" Declan asked, extending his hand.

"Yup."

"I used to be with Third," Rex said. "Got out in 2000. Separated after six years. Made Captain. Then punched out."

"Rex Bowbart?" Hooch's dark eyes widened. "Hey, Brother! We went through SERE together."

"Man, I thought I recognized you." Rex hugged him. "How the hell are you?"

"Everything's good other than having to deal with those yahoos." Hooch pointed toward the TOC. "So, when did you get in country?"

There was no need for any rapport building with Hooch and Griff. Rex came through again, and Declan was amazed at how many contacts his team leader had in this small part of the world.

"A couple of weeks ago." Rex replied as they neared his office. "You guys wanna come in for a bit?" His breath fogged the night air.

Hooch looked to Griff. "Sure."

"Can I get you something to drink?" Declan asked.

"We're good, thanks."

Someone knocked on the door. So much for reminiscing about old times. Declan opened it, Captain Jack and two companions appeared. The team room quickly filled with bodies.

"Well, look at what the cat dragged in." Rex laughed.

"We need to find a way to stay clear of those meetings," Captain

Jack said. "Let me introduce you guys to Shrek and Tattoo. They're my go-to guys. Ever need anything and I'm not around, they'll help you out."

The men bonded almost instantly, and the energy level was high. Declan realized he wasn't the only one thinking outside the box. Rex had a master plan this entire time, and it was unfolding perfectly. The only person missing to make the introductions complete was Baba Rich from the Haj.

Rex knew what he was doing, though, by excluding Baba Rich for now. Whether he would be accepted by the group remained questionable. He was a former Marine officer turned NGO, and everyone knew there was a rift between NGOs and the military. It wasn't wise to test anyone's loyalties at this point.

Just as the conversations rose in volume again, another knock pounded at the door.

"Who is it?" Rex asked.

"C'mon, Rex, let me in."

The door opened, and Major Franks appeared. A tall man with dark hair, he always wore US Army, standard-issued birth control glasses—the type that no woman would find sexy. He loosely toted his 9mm in his shoulder holster to make him feel more manly, knowing he would never use the damn thing since he was an office jockey never meant to leave the wire. He was the Brigade public affairs officer and much more academic than soldier. Incredibly annoying too.

"You guys are having a party and didn't invite me?" he asked.

"Sorry, Major," Rex said. "We thought you only enjoyed tea parties."

He grabbed an old leather football. Declan felt himself grin. Every time Rex needed to think long and hard, every time someone annoying came into the office, that football was his outlet.

Contracted: America's Secret Warriors

"Very funny," the Major said. "So what's going on?"

Around the room, a bunch of beards stared toward the ground, and Declan knew he wasn't the only one with hostility toward the Major.

"Having a serious meeting right now, Major." Rex spiraled the ball above his head.

"Oh, what are you guys discussing? Maybe I can add some insight."

"Sorry, Major, this is closed-door stuff."

"You're no fun." He hung his head like a child being scolded. "I see how you guys are."

Finally, he turned to leave.

"Damn," Rex said, once the door had fully closed behind the Major. "Can't he ever take a hint?"

"Actually, I think he might be the smartest guy on this base," Declan told him. "He knows we're up to something, and that's why he tries coming in here every hour."

"Up to something?" Griff asked. "What's that mean?"

"How good is your HUMINT, Griff?" Declan asked.

"HUMINT? You mean interrogations or walk-ins?" Griff placed some Copenhagen in his mouth.

"Exactly." Declan blurted. "Intel here sucks. All they do here is SIGINT. That isn't getting them anywhere. They need real, outside-the-box human intelligence."

"There're already teams established for that type of work." Griff reached for an empty paper cup to spit into.

"No. You know the reality behind those teams. No one's doing real HUMINT, where guys go out in local garb without any security details, live with the locals, and do real source operations filled with heavy unconventional trade craft."

"Hold on, fellas," Hooch interjected. "What you're talking about can't be done. DOD set up too many rules. State would go berserk if they ever caught wind, and OGA would kill you if they ever found out you had any contact with any of their sources."

Declan threw the old pigskin back to his partner, knowing Rex would ease Hooch's concerns.

"State Department has their heads so far up their asses, they'd never have a clue what's going on." Rex eyed them as if making sure everyone paid close attention. "When I was on active duty, I learned real quick that the Army has a waiver for everything. Colonel Davis already approved Dec and me to disappear until next Friday. He was smart enough not to ask any questions. OGA, well, they're more concerned about the other side of the border. I doubt they're running too many sources on this side."

Captain Jack didn't say a word. It was as if he had already opted into the plan with Rex earlier. Shrek and Tattoo were also quietly on board. Hooch absorbed everything Rex had just pitched, and Griff appeared perplexed that two civilians who had so recently arrived in country could be so serious.

"Who the hell do you two work for?" Griff demanded.

"Really?" Declan replied, "You know who we are. We're military advisors."

In war, it is often best not to ask too many questions, and clearly Hooch was aware of that. "OK, so you two are going out for a week?" he asked.

"Yup." Rex self-passed the ball in the air.

"So what do you guys need from us, Rex?"

"Right now, nothing. Will we probably need you later? Yup."

"Just remember, if you guys get in trouble, we can't just go off the yard anytime we want to be your quick reaction force," Hooch replied.

"We'd be dead before any team like that could get close enough to help us out," Declan said. "We'll need to collaborate our intel with you guys, fuse everything we have into the bigger picture."

"A fusion cell already exists next to the TOC," Griff said.

"Yup. It does, but it's not complete," Declan explained. "And what we're about to do will make it complete for when you walk in there next week, Griff. After we get back."

Another knock came to the door. The conversation immediately ceased. In came Major Franks once again.

"Saw your light was still on, so I figured I would just stop by before I headed out for the night."

"Sleep in the Stan is overrated, Major," Rex said.

"Meeting over yet?"

"Well, everyone's still here, so what do you think?" Rex asked. "How did you ever make Major with those kinds of questions anyway?"

"God, Rex, you're such a dick."

"Sorry, sir, I didn't mean to make you cry."

Declan shook his head and thought, *just leave before Rex mind-rapes you.*

"Anyone know what time the locals clean the latrines at night?" Rex paused for a second, allowing the Major to wonder where he was going with his question. "I think the Major just wanted to come back in here to check me out before he takes his evening cold shower. I wouldn't go in the latrines until after the locals clean them."

Everyone in the room burst out in laughter. Griff laughed so hard that he swallowed his dip. Declan had never seen a field-grade officer get abused so badly.

Looking pissed, Major Franks stalked out. The door slammed shut, nearly rattling the walls.

"Like a kid with a temper tantrum," Rex said.

"A bit rough on the guy, don't you think?" Declan put the football down on the floor. Rex went after it.

"Screw him. He's like a woman. I can only take so much of him in one day."

"Hence, why you're not married."

"Whatever."

Declan was getting tired. Tomorrow would be exciting, with Rex and him moving out to a new temporary home at the Haj. "So, is everyone on board?"

It was clear that everyone was indeed on board. Rex seemed pleased. Captain Jack and his team stood and walked out the door, followed by Hooch and Griff. Rex closed down his computer and began to follow everyone else's lead.

"You coming?" he asked.

"I'll be right behind you." Declan reached into his pocket to grab his daily-use cell phone. "Gonna call Bran real quick."

"Roger that. Tell her to start scoping out one of her single friends for me."

"Her friends are all married."

"She's a teacher, for God's sake. There must be some single chicks in her school."

"I'll see what she can do."

But all he was really thinking about was the comforting sound of Bran's voice. Declan loved hearing her speak. It made him remember what waited for him at home, and listening to her, for even a moment, was the one thing that brought him happiness over here.

SEVEN

T ourniquets, gauze, bandages, chitosan, and other medical supplies, including ibuprofen and antacids, were scattered on the floor. Declan knew he was going outside the wire for several days without significant support. What little medical supplies he could pack could be lifesavers.

When Rex walked into the office, his face showed that he liked what he saw. He opened a closet and pulled out some extra supplies. "Here, see if you have any room for any of this."

Rex's cell rang. It was Baba Rich. Relaying the quick conversation, Rex said, "He's on his way now. He'll be here in about fifteen."

Declan didn't answer. He was too focused on ensuring everything they could possibly need was packed. The med kit was stuffed to full capacity. They sealed it and ran through their checklist of supplies.

An assortment of batteries, hundred-mile-an-hour tape, five-fifty cord, headlamps with red and blue lenses, notepads, pencils and pens, digital cameras, and recording devices. They were all part of the essentials.

"Going out in the field, and this is the first time I actually didn't pack more than three pairs of socks." Rex looked down at his huge feet.

"Yup. Going Afghan style seems to lighten the load quite a bit." Declan glanced down at his own bare feet protected by open-toe leather sandals.

"I can actually get used to these man-jammies." Rex checked himself out in the local shalwar kameez clothing through a small hand mirror. The light blue pants and top and midnight blue Afghan vest contrasted with his milk-white skin. He could easily pass for one of the remaining fair-skinned Russians from the 1980s Russian Afghan War.

Declan looked back down and didn't comment. He was focused on getting off the FOB without anyone like Major Franks seeing them leave. He would ask questions, too many questions, and likely run to the Brigade commander, crying about two civilians running off the yard.

"Hey, can you open the locker and pull out the AKs?" Declan asked.

Rex pulled out two Kalashnikov AKMS assault rifles and a stack of thirty-round magazines. "Captain Jack really hooked us up with these. Folding stocks, Picatinny rails, EOTech sites. These are too sweet."

Declan heard the rare sound of a vehicle outside the office and knew it was Baba Rich. No one else had the balls to drive wherever they wanted on the yard.

Rex peeked outside the door. "He's here. You ready?"

"Let's go."

Baba Rich was decked out. In his shalwar kameez and Pashtun-style Pakol hat, he looked more Pashtun than American. Declan hoped he looked as good in the eyes of the locals.

"Damn!" Baba Rich braked as he unlocked the passenger side door. "You guys fit right in."

If Declan had any worries about blending in, those worries were gone. Fifteen minutes to the Haj. Eyes needed to stay focused, looking for any roadside IEDs or worse, an approaching VBIED.

Baba Rich appeared excited to have some additional muscle by his side, instead of the normal NGOs he was used to dealing with. "Got some good news for you guys," he said. "Spoke with Haji Haq this morning. Got it all set up where we can head to his old man's district so I can introduce you two to his dad."

"Go to the Haj first or go straight to his location?" Rex asked as he placed his weapon across his lap

"No need to waste any time at the Haj."

There they were, Declan thought. Three American men mirroring the locals in appearance only were loaded up and heading into the wild of Afghanistan. In Baba Rich's white Toyota pickup, they departed to see one of eastern Afghanistan's most respected warriors, a true legend. Declan was amped and excited to finally do his job.

After an hour of weaving in and out of city traffic, they pulled off on a desolate dirt road. The change was refreshing. Declan felt alive. He was on sensory overload.

Then he saw them. Three men were perched on a nearby hilltop, with AKs shouldered and ICOM radios in their hands.

"Spotters. Two o'clock," he said, fearing an ambush.

"Good eyes." Rex, ready to fight if needed, turned his head in the opposite direction, gripping his AK. "Two more. Fifty meters. Ten o'clock."

"They're Haq's men," Baba Rich said and accelerated. "Relax. He has an army. They knew we were coming. They're protecting us right now."

"Protecting us?" Declan asked, searching for any enemy activity.

"If anyone made the mistake of following or trying to ambush us, Haq's men will kill them." Baba repositioned himself in his driver's seat, maintaining a better grip on the steering wheel.

"How many guys does Haq have?" Rex glanced out the rear

window, ensuring no one followed them.

"Two hundred at any given time." Baba Rich flashed his headlights, signaling the guards at a makeshift checkpoint up ahead. "If he needs more, he has access to thousands. He's in good with about fifty former Muj who all have their own little armies."

"So you weren't blowing smoke when you described this guy." Rex continued checking out the surroundings. "The Mujahideen are some tough bastards."

At the checkpoint, the guards waved them through. Baba Rich didn't even bring the vehicle to a halt. He knew the ins-and-outs of this place better than anyone.

"This is Afghanistan," he said. "The only smoke being blown here is from dust storms and explosions."

"You put a lot of trust in these people." Declan meant it as a comment more than a question.

"You have to. No army ever made it out of Afghanistan victoriously. If they wanted me dead, I would have been long ago. I have something they want, and they have something I want. We play the game, make friendships on the way, and everyone goes home at the end of the night with all their fingers and toes."

"That's you," Rex said. "But will they feel that way about Dec and me?"

"Oh, you guys?" Baba Rich laughed. "No, you guys are dead. I'm bringing you to them as a gift. You know, kind of like an old Aztec sacrifice, but Afghan style."

"Nice," Rex said.

"OK, we're here. Don't forget, this guy is the real deal. Even the Taliban fear him. Be respectful, all right? None of that conventional Army bullshit."

"Don't worry. We're not in the military," Declan reminded him.

"Yeah, I know. Just don't forget it while you're speaking to him. No machismo crap."

Baba Rich put the truck in park.

"Baba," Declan said, "you got to admit that it's a bit funny hearing a retired Marine officer speak like that about the military."

"You were Air Force, right? Shoot, that means you weren't even in the military." Baba Rich took the keys out of the ignition. "I'm only kidding about that, but if you saw what I have from those clowns in the past two years I've been here, you'd probably feel the same way."

Declan was on an adrenaline high. He ignored the conversation, knowing it needed to end. He didn't appreciate the military bashing especially when the majority of troops were making the best out of a bad situation run politically amok. It was game time anyway. His recording device ready, he strategically placed it inside a homemade holster concealed in his waistband.

"Rex, you got quiet. Everything all right?"

"Hell yeah. Just needed to put my game face on."

Declan took a deep breath and tried to calm himself. Even with Baba Rich's confidence, he was nervous. The only thing he could do now was play the game and hope to come out on top.

EIGHT

A herd of Afghan villagers swarmed Baba Rich. They loved the guy, Declan thought. All Declan could hear were tiny voices chirping like baby birds, *treat, treat, treat.* Boys and girls alike adored this character the villagers had nicknamed "the Candy Man."

Declan and the men were greeted with traditional Afghan hugs and kisses from the Afghan men. Haq's men shuffled them over to a courtyard in the middle of the village.

Sitting underneath the shade of a tree was Mehsud Haq, an Afghan legend.

Declan was amazed at the size and stature of the man. Six-feet plus, he was tall for an Afghan. Sporting a salt-and-pepper beard with much more salt in it than pepper, Haq had skin that looked like leather from years of working in the Afghan sun. His hands were large and strong. His English reflected his years spent in Texas, where he was trained to be a CIA asset during the Russian Afghan War.

"It's so nice to meet you," Declan said. "Rich told us many good things about you."

"Yes. And not one of them is true." Mr. Haq smiled and showed brown teeth.

"Men, this guy is a legend," Baba Rich interjected. "Listen and learn. He'll tell you everything you ever needed to know about Afghanistan."

"Come. I had lunch prepared for your arrival." Haq moved the men into the center of the courtyard, where traditional Afghan food was displayed on a handmade blanket on the ground. "We can talk about business later."

It was a feast consisting of Afghan flat bread, goat, rice, fresh fruits, and vegetables. Twelve men sat around the food in no particular order, passing a pitcher of water among them. Each poured a mild stream of water into their filth-covered hands, letting it flow into a small bowl below. The single drying towel was filthy. Declan hesitated as the others shoved their dirty hands into the food trays. *Dear God, don't let me get some parasite or dysentery. Why didn't I pack any Cipro tabs?*

"What is this?" Declan asked as a bowl with a milky substance was passed around. Each man who touched the beverage drank from the bowl. "Goat milk?"

"Dogh." Mr. Haq answered. "It's like liquid yogurt."

"I don't know if I can do this," Declan whispered over to Rex. "It's warm."

"Drink it."

Declan picked up the bowl, allowing the warm substance to touch his lips without entering his mouth. Quickly, before anyone could suggest that he drink more, he handed the bowl over to Rex. "Your turn."

Rex drank enough for him and his cowardly partner. "This is an incredible feast. Thank you."

Declan's first feast in Afghanistan could have fed an entire army. Once he was able to get over the lack of sanitary conditions, he was able to enjoy the meal.

"Is this a daily occurrence?"

Pieces of food stuck to Mr. Haq's beard as he ate like a savage. "This is normally our dinner. But this is what we do for guests."

"Well, we cannot thank you enough."

After the feast, Mr. Haq led them to a shaded stream nearby. Inviting all to take a seat, Haq became the teacher, and Declan his student.

Hours passed, and history unfolded. Haq told many stories about his fights against the Russians. He told them with pride, and Declan was impressed.

"Taliban today, they are cowards. They do not know how to fight." Haq placed a pinch of green naswar tobacco between his lips and gums.

Declan couldn't resist himself and he broke out laughing.

"Wow, people even dip in Afghanistan." He took out a can of Skoal. "Have you ever tried American tobacco?"

"Declan, everything in Afghanistan is strong. American tobacco is weak. Want to try some of mine?"

"Thank you, sir, but I'll pass. I don't know if I'm man enough yet." Everyone began to laugh. Mr. Haq clearly loved the company and being the forefront of attention.

One of Haq's armed guards rushed over to the stream. Declan couldn't make out anything being said, and Haq's amiable expression quickly turned disgruntled.

"What is it?" Baba Rich asked.

"It's getting late." Haq stood. "I don't believe it's safe for you to leave tonight."

"You want us to stay?" Rex appeared unfazed as he threw a pebble into the flowing stream. "I'm cool with that."

"Stay?" Declan was hesitant.

While the villagers were welcoming, staying inside an Afghan village with just two other Americans sounded like a mistake. He didn't like what was unfolding.

"C'mon, it's like going camping," Rex said, "but we're protected by the baddest men who ever walked this earth. I'm more comfortable here than on base or at the Haj."

After a moment passed, Declan agreed. They were in a safe place. Baba Rich had spent many nights in Haq's village and never had a problem. First light, they could leave.

"Yeah, why not? It'll be an adventure, to say the least."

"Mehsud, so what's actually going on?" Baba Rich asked as they began walking back to the village interior.

"Mullah Bhetani's men set up surveillance on the Torkham Highway," Mr. Haq explained. "They have plans to conduct a kidnapping of American NGOs. I can't allow anything happening to you. You're my responsibility."

While unnerved by the news, Declan appreciated Mr. Haq's resolve. He looked over at Rex. "Should I let Griff know about this?"

"No. Call Captain Jack instead. Let him know what's going on. Have him pass word over to the Third Group guys."

Declan made the call. Jack sounded amused by the situation.

"Hanging around Rex will likely increase your chances of complex adventures," he said.

"Yeah, I can see that as we go along."

"Whatever you do, listen to what he says," Jack told him. "He's a survivor, and he knows how to work independently. If I don't hear from you by morning, I'll round up the guys and formulate a strategy."

"Thanks for having our backs," Declan said. "I'm glad we can count on you guys."

In the back of his mind, death was always knocking. It would take only one stray bullet to end everything. If Jack didn't hear from them, he would execute a search. That was the only comfort Declan found in the situation: if things got ugly, his body wouldn't be left behind.

NINE

D eclan loved experiencing new cultures and new people. Staying the night in an Afghan village would take him to the next level.

Mehsud Haq escorted the men around the village, showing them where everything they would need to be comfortable throughout the night was located. An outside commode was situated in the immediate vicinity of Haq's home—indoor plumbing was hundreds of years from the Pashtun's current time.

Due to cultural differences, Declan and his partners would never step foot inside Haq's living space. He had a wife, a daughter, and a son. The non-Islamic Americans could not see the women unless they were fully covered from head to toe. Inside the Afghan home, the women dressed casually as seeing outsiders was not a threat.

However, Haq had a guestroom near the front door of his home. It was connected to the house, but excluding the mud walls, it was more like an American sunroom, and completely unfurnished except for some pillows on the ground. Haq promised some mattresses for their comfort.

When everything was situated, the men walked back outside near the center of the village where a warm fire blazed. It was story time again.

"Mehsud, tell them about some of the times you fought the Russians." Baba Rich loved hearing about the Russians being decimated by Afghan tribesmen.

"They were some of the fiercest warriors Afghanistan ever encountered." Haq sat on a blanket close to the fire. "They were very different than the Americans."

"How so?" Declan asked as he took his seat.

"Americans are stupid. They continue to go into villages that have no meaning. There is no value in a lot of what you do."

"And the Russians didn't go into some of those villages?" Declan was a bit confused.

"Americans go into places like the Pesh River and Korengal River valleys. You go into places like Nuristan." Haq continued with his astute observations of military strategy. "Russians tried that briefly and realized fast that they would never gain or keep any ground. So they concentrated on the places they knew they could win. The Russians were fierce. They would bomb us night and day. Americans go and build us things and all the while, the Taliban shoots at them. It makes no sense. How could we respect a people who won't kill?"

"You don't think the Americans kill Afghans?" Rex jumped in. "Don't you think we killed enough people to prove our willingness to take Afghan lives?"

"No." Haq immediately disagreed. "If you fight a war, you must win by pure might. You must saturate the air with bullets and bombs. Women, children, men of old and young, they must all die. Sooner or later, the people will turn on your enemy and fight with you. But they won't do this until you prove you're willing to kill everyone."

"American news would have a field day with that approach." Declan began to chuckle. "That tactic wouldn't go over too well with the American people or the international community for that matter."

"And that is why America is weak." Haq smiled. "Americans care too much about what others think of them. This makes you weak. In fact, the only reason your people still remain alive here in Afghanistan is because you are people of faith where the Russians weren't. We crushed the Russians and they were much fiercer than the Americans."

"People of faith? Russians don't believe in God? Is that what you mean?" Rex seemed alarmed. "Russians believe in God, Mr. Haq."

"No, they are communists. It's against communist doctrine to believe in God," Haq protested.

Baba looked over to Rex with a stern look. His facial expression communicated it well: *Let it go, Rex.*

As Rex quieted, one of Haq's men walked over to the fire. He held a small book in one hand and a folder in the other.

"This book was written long ago by one of your universities." Haq handed the booklet to Rex first so he could examine what was inside.

"University of Nebraska-Omaha…USAID…1983," Rex muttered beneath his breath. "Holy crap."

"What is it, Rex?" Declan asked.

"It's a propaganda piece." Baba explained. "It was one of the first things Haq showed me when I first met him. Skim through it and you'll see why so many Islamists hate us."

Declan was quick to look over Rex's shoulder, and the two examined the book through the shimmer from the fire.

"If two infidels stand, and one is killed by a Mujahideen, how many infidels are left to be killed?" Rex read from one of the math lessons found in the book. "This is supposed to be a school book?"

"Yup." Baba hung his head low. "During the Russian war, the US furnished Afghanistan with these types of books. They included loads of hate and propaganda to fuel the Afghan inferno which sparked Islamic radicalization."

"So this is how Afghanistan became radicalized?" Declan asked. "I remember seeing photos of Afghan women in Kabul in the 60s and 70s wearing mini-skirts. Stuff like this is what changed all that?"

"You could say so." Rex lifted his head and looked over to Mr. Haq. "And with such a low literacy rate, and little communication with the outside world, why wouldn't they believe these types of things?"

"Your propaganda didn't just come through books," Haq noted. "You brought Afghans like me to the United States. Some of us were trained by your military, others by your CIA, and a few by your universities. We came back preaching what we learned in your country."

"And the biggest lesson was that Russians were not good people. They didn't believe in God, they were infidels," Declan stated and felt a chill from the cooling night air.

"Now you see why Islamists roam Afghanistan," Haq concluded. "We can't blame America fully. But you are partly to be blamed."

"So the United States created a monster it no longer has any control over." Declan felt defeated.

"Yes, you could say America destroyed what Afghanistan once was. But, in this folder, I have something that could change all that."

"What's in it?" Rex asked.

"You two are going to shit yourselves when you see this," Baba blurted. "Haq is like a manager of a professional baseball team."

"What do you mean?"

Haq opened the folder. In it were several pieces of paper and a list of hundreds of names—all in English. Were the Taliban to find Haq's secret document, they would need time to translate and identify all the persons written in it.

"This is my plan to save Afghanistan and defeat the Taliban." Haq smiled as if he were a mastermind. "These names are warlords I am friends with throughout the country. They are waiting for the Americans to allow me to execute my plan."

"Explain," Rex wanted more. He found great interest in Afghan strategies.

"All these men have little armies. If the Americans allow us to become recognized, we can form our own guard force in our districts and throughout our provinces."

"Kind of like our National Guard?" Rex asked.

"These forces would be controlled only by the warlords and the village elders would approve their operations," Haq continued. "All we need is our weapons back. The weapons your state department took from us."

The plan reminded Declan of the meeting with the village elders from the Mohmand Tribe. Haq had just confirmed that this was what many warlords wished for. It was a plan that could save American lives.

"So you want the Americans to provide you with weapons, ammunition, and training?" Declan suggested.

"Weapons and ammunition, yes." Haq shook his head. "Training, no. We don't need your training."

"Why would you not want our training?" asked Rex.

"We are better foot soldiers than the Americans. We don't need all the technology the American military needs. We can navigate through the desert and forest without a compass. We can move in the night by following the stars. And we have been trained in tactics from hundreds of years of outsiders wishing to take our lands."

"He's got a point, Rex." Declan smiled with delight at such honesty. "The US would waste a lot of money and resources training the

Afghans when truth is, they do a good job fighting already."

They heard commotion a brief distance away. Villagers started to gather near the front of the compound. Tension filled the air.

Mehsud Haq rose to his feet and calmly walked toward the crowd. Baba followed as did Declan and Rex. Could this be further insight about the Taliban's threat to kidnap American NGOs?

A young boy was the center of attention. He had tears in his eyes. The boy's frantic appearance was much more than alarm over losing his favorite teddy bear. Declan could not understand his Pashtu but Baba captured bits and pieces.

"Taliban approached the boy," Baba explained. "He's scared."

"What'd they say?" Rex asked. "Did they hurt him?"

"It'll be all right," Mr. Haq stated as he turned to face his American guests. "We need to put the three of you to bed for the night."

The situation did not call for any explanation. The air was strained and Declan knew he was at the mercy of Haq and his villagers' kindness.

The men walked back to Haq's guest room. Mattresses were placed on the floor as promised. This would be home for the night.

"Don't know about you guys, but I'm sleeping with one eye open." Rex chuckled to himself.

"No need for that," Baba interjected. "We take turns pulling watch. We'll rotate every hour pulling shift. I'll go first so I can try to hear anything about what just happened. "

"Makes sense to me." However, Declan knew better than to let his guard down, his adrenaline making it difficult to sleep.

Sometime throughout the night, Declan managed to succumb to much needed rest. But no sooner than his eyes had fully closed, he felt a clammy hand on his shoulder.

Declan's eyes opened wide. He didn't say a word. Hovering above him was a ghostly pale figure surrounded by the moonlight shining through the open window of the room. It was Rex, with his index finger lightly placed over his mouth.

Voices could be heard through the open window. Baba, Rex, and Declan peeked outside to see a familiar face. Mr. Haq was surrounded by his guard force, confronted by a small contingent of Taliban.

"They know we're here," Baba whispered. "They're saying something about the boy from earlier told them we were here."

Rex was quick to pull out the weapon he had concealed throughout the day. It was only a 9mm pistol, but he wasn't going down without a fight.

"Stand down, Rex," Baba demanded in a quiet tone. "They'll have to kill Haq and all his men to get to us."

"You sure about that?" asked Declan.

Baba didn't need to say anything. He beamed his eyes down on Declan and Rex and the two knew he was right. Haq was an honorable man, a man who lived by the Pashtun honor code—Pashtunwali. They were his guests and he was obligated to protect them.

A shouting match ensued outside. Haq reminded Declan of a true warrior. His tall figure superseded the others. His grim face needed no war paint. He would handle the situation.

In a matter of minutes, the Taliban turned away from the village empty handed. No words were spoken between Haq and his armed guards.

The wooden door of Mr. Haq's house creaked open. He calmly walked into the guest room where the Americans were staying.

"As the sun begins to rise, my men will escort you out of the area," he explained. "Get some rest."

Haq didn't wait for any comment. He turned and walked toward the entry of his living quarters. Nothing more needed to be said: Taliban knew that three Americans stayed at the village. The village was no longer safe.

His back turned to the doorway, Haq stopped and looked back at his American guests. His face was stern. His eyes were red with anger.

"That boy is my nephew. They beat him with sticks so he would speak. He didn't mean to tell them you were here. I ask that you forgive him for jeopardizing your safety. But know you are still safe."

"No, Mr. Haq, it was our presence that caused your nephew to face the brutality of the Taliban," Baba expressed himself.

"They caused a war by touching him," Mr. Haq noted with bold articulation. "And they will pay. The right time will come, and they will be punished."

Mehsud Haq continued inside his living quarters, saying nothing more. It was no time to converse and the Americans knew it. During the French and Indian wars, the enemy was prone to attack an hour before dawn and an hour after dusk. All the troops would pull watch, leaving no one asleep. This was called stand-two. Declan and his team would pull stand-two the remainder of the night. Luckily for them, the Taliban never came back.

These were the types of dangers Declan knew he would face serving in Afghanistan. They were dangers that often came with disastrous outcomes or magnificent results. If Declan could get back to base alive, he could divulge everything Haq revealed to decision makers. Haq had a plan to bring peace to Afghanistan. It was a plan that made sense to Declan and Rex. It was a plan that could save lives.

TEN

T heir night with Mehsud Haq ended. The early morning Afghan sun had risen high above the mountainous terrain. Children, dressed in their brightly colored traditional Afghan garb, were off doing chores around the village. No time for a morning cup of chai. Declan, Baba Rich, and Rex needed to return to the Haj.

They exchanged cell numbers. Then they hugged and shook hands as they said their goodbyes. Mr. Haq offered his village to them at any time they desired in the future.

"We are all warriors only separated by our mothers," he said.

Rex had awakened in his normal jovial mood. "That's right, Mr. Haq. We're brothers from another mother."

Haq was confused by the comment but knew it was a gesture of agreement. Declan nudged his buddy into the car, worried he may unintentionally say something that would upset their host.

"Thank you for allowing us to stay." Declan climbed into the pickup. "We'll stay in touch."

"If you ever need me, or my men, know we are here to help." Mr. Haq waved goodbye.

The team drove off as two vehicles full of Haq's armed guards led the way. The escort could only go so far, as Haq's domain was limited. Still, Declan appreciated the armed escort.

"Damn, was that one wild night or what?" Rex laid his AK-47 across his lap.

"No television show or movie could ever compete with the entertainment we just had." Declan angled the muzzle of his weapon near the door.

"Told you guys," Baba Rich said from behind the wheel. "That guy is the real deal."

"He's more than that." Declan observed a cloud of dust from a vehicle nearing them. "He's an intelligence gold mine. That's what he is."

Rich took a hard left onto the hardball.

"I have some friends coming over tonight," he said. "It's not the typical Thursday shindig, but I think you guys will appreciate these folks."

"Afghans?" Rex asked.

"No. Some NGOs."

"I highly doubt they'll be as entertaining as Mr. Haq."

Declan watched a three-wheeled, rickshaw-type vehicle loaded with four women wearing light blue burqas pass by. He believed the women in Afghanistan were treated like modern-day slaves, and the women he saw were likely being shipped off to their masters.

"Don't underestimate the NGOs here," Baba Rich said. "While their jobs may not be to collect intelligence, their lives depend on it, and they're good at it too."

The vehicle went silent. Haq's guards veered off as they reached their limit, about ten miles away from Baba's safe house. Declan's team needed to stay focused until they reached the Haj. Traveling to and from the home in Afghanistan came with grave risks. Declan and Rex knew that. Baba Rich knew too. For the remainder of the ride, Baba explained how he'd been hit by an IED in Iraq back in 2003.

"We're here!" Baba Rich sounded excited that he had made it back to his home safely.

It was already steaming hot outside. Upon exiting the truck, Rex didn't speak. He ran over to the pool and did a giant cannon ball. Declan knew from a few nights back that the pool was filled with piss-warm water. Before he could say a word, Baba Rich followed Rex's lead. Declan realized that the pool wasn't really about cooling off. It served as a sign of comfort: they had avoided danger while being outside the wire.

A few hours passed. The three of them sat poolside, bathing in the Afghan sun, wearing just their skivvies. Evening came, and an Afghan housemaid served up some grub. Fire roasted goat alongside bouranee baunjan, an eggplant dish that came with yogurt. Gulpea, a delicious cauliflower dish complemented the meal. They ate and then prepared for an evening with Rich's NGO acquaintances, which included Dr. James, who looked more like an American soap opera doctor than the real thing. Even his five o'clock shadow was fashionable.

Declan realized that alcohol took two forms in their lives. Scotch for serious occasions. It was always strictly business. Rum and coke for playtime. This was a rum-and-coke night.

Six NGOs entered the Haj and made their way to the tiki bar, where Declan was pouring warm cola into equally warm rum they had purchased at the embassy in Kabul. Ice was a commodity he'd already learned to live without.

"How sad that the military can't drink, but the embassy has a stash of this stuff," Declan said.

"It's a dog-eat-dog world, my friend." Rex toasted him.

"Dr. James." Declan placed his glass down. "Thought you went into Pakistan."

"Just came back from a Taliban-controlled hospital there." Dr. James grabbed himself a warm brew from behind the bar.

"We haven't seen you since you first introduced us to Rich," Rex said. "By the way, what do you mean Taliban-controlled?"

"Yup. They allow me access, knowing that I have supplies and am the only real doctor in the region."

"You got to be kidding me?"

"I run a bunch of Iraqi nurses over there." James took a quick swig. "They're Christians, but the Taliban doesn't know that. They're my life line."

"Bullshit," Rex uttered.

"No, he's serious." Baba Rich left the pool where the other NGOs sat. "Show them the pictures."

Dr. James took out his laptop. He opened a file of pictures displaying the hospital, then pointed to a few key, injured Taliban receiving treatment there.

"Holy crap." Declan was amazed. "And they allowed these photos?"

"No way. They would kill me if they knew I took them. This is what I use." The doc pulled out a micro camera easily hidden inside a pen. "I take the photos then write down their names."

"I gotta ask a dumb question." Rex refilled his glass as he promoted himself to bartender. "Does anyone in the IC know you have this stuff?"

"I tried working with some folks in the intel community, but they got too pushy." The doc placed his beer on the table as he closed down his computer. "I was hoping that eventually someone like you two would come around."

"What do you mean too pushy?" Declan asked.

"You know." With beer in hand again, Dr. James explained. "They want to tell me when, where, with whom, etc. I don't work like that. I want to stay alive. I know how to do things my way."

"Who taught you?" Declan was in disbelief. "I mean, who taught you how to operate?"

"Self-taught. I've been doing this for years down in South America, Africa, and now here in the Stan." James reached into his backpack and handed over a thumb drive. "This has a file in it. Filled with photos of high-value targets and their names."

"That easy?" Rex asked. "What's the catch?"

"No catch. I'm an American. I do this because I'm a patriot. I hate seeing our kids get killed."

"But you're willing to help the enemy?" Rex poured another drink.

"No, Rex." Declan took the glass from his buddy. "What he gives is nothing compared to what he gets in return. That's what the art is all about."

Declan realized that hanging around Baba Rich was an exceptional position. In just twenty-four hours, he had met an Afghan legend who was willing to support Rex and him, and he had met a crazy doctor who had intel unlike anything seen back on the FOB. Declan believed this was exactly what he was intended to do. He felt unstoppable.

ELEVEN

D ays passed, and Declan couldn't have felt any better. The Haj turned out to be the honeypot he had imagined. He and Rex had discovered the missing link of intelligence in Afghanistan, intelligence that could only be found in the Haj. He was confident Colonel Davis would see the value in keeping the two of them off the yard.

Photos of high-value targets that could be identified by name was something the US intelligence operating in Afghanistan was missing. They lacked images that would ensure positive identification upon their capture. The images James had hand-delivered were invaluable.

Meeting with warlords who welcomed the American presence offered a human intelligence source with potential to pass along village secrets. Or better, pass along actionable intelligence they received from their own intelligence networks.

Did they know how to operate more effectively than the US military? Whether they did mattered little. Their ideas should be considered by decision makers if this war were truly to be conducted as a unified coalition—including the locals during counterinsurgency operations is critical and to date, the US hadn't played that game very well.

The Haj was indeed a honey hole. It was a centralized location flooded with untapped information. Information that was critical for fusion operations, operations where intelligence officers "fused" all the different insights on the ground into one big package of understanding.

US Army personnel on the FOB worked diligently. Declan saw

everyone's movements as a sign of enlightenment. But four helicopters—red crosses painted on their sides—approached the base tarmac, and Declan's high spirits immediately vanished. The presence of the choppers likely indicated US casualties.

"Let's go straight to the TOC," Rex said as his pace quickened into double time.

"This isn't good." Declan joined Rex. "We step back on the yard and casualties come in."

Toting AKs, kit bags, and wearing Afghan man-jammies, he and Rex entered the tactical operations center. It was packed, and Declan felt all the eyes inside stare as they came in.

Colonel Davis spotted them. He hurried them into his office and closed the door behind him.

"When you leave here, take that local crap off immediately and change," he ordered.

"Roger that, sir." Declan sat in attention, knowing the environment within the TOC wasn't good.

"What's going on, Colonel?" Rex asked.

"What's going on?" With a pen in hand, he began pointing to the Korengal Valley in the Kunar Province. "We just got our asses handed to us."

"How bad?" Declan asked.

"We just had an outpost overrun." Colonel Davis took a seat behind his desk. "An entire squad was taken out, twelve men. All but two of the bodies were recovered. Everything stops in this AO until I get my two men accounted for."

"Sir, what do you need us to do?" Rex studied the map posted on the wall. "Anything you need, sir."

"First thing I need is for you two avatars to get dressed. Put on some real pants and shirts. Look like my advisors, and not some blood-thirsty, Taliban-loving assholes!"

This was the first time Declan had seen the colonel so furious. "Give us ten minutes, sir. We have clothes in our team room. We'll be right back."

They left the office swiftly. Rex, having been through similar situations while working in Iraq, wouldn't allow the tragedy to bring him down. Declan followed his lead.

"Well?" he asked Rex as they entered their team room. "Do we even attempt to discuss the intel we have with the colonel when we get back?"

"Are you nuts?" Rex replied. He seemed to change as fast as Clark Kent in a telephone booth. "No, we get our asses back in there and don't say a word until we're asked to speak."

"An entire squad…" Declan uttered as he laced up his boots.

"It's not about the squad as much as it is about having two men unaccounted for," Rex replied as he opened the door. "Be prepared. Brigade is likely to shift all focus on Kunar."

"So does that mean we place everything on hold?" Declan stood as he headed toward the door.

"We'll see. I need to speak with Jack when we get out of the TOC." Rex ushered him out the door. "C'mon, we need to go."

Declan entered the TOC. This time the chaos continued uninterrupted when they entered. Declan was stressed just looking at the commotion.

"My two military advisors!" Colonel Davis waved them forward. "How I missed you two."

"In a better mood?" Rex asked.

"Dr. Rex." Davis had a huge grin on his face. "You played football in college. What's a team to do when they're down by a field goal with only two minutes left, and the ball is on their own twenty-yard line?"

Rex thought for a second "A two-minute drill?"

"That's right. And what's so special about a two-minute drill, Dr. Rex?" the colonel asked in a quasi-condescending way. "I'll answer for you. In a two-minute drill, you put your fastest men on the field, your most conditioned men, who know what urgency really means, men who fully grasp the term execution."

"Yes, sir, I understand."

"Come on, gents. We need to go to the briefing room and have a makeshift huddle. We're planning our two-minute drill."

Declan followed the two men next door. The small space was filled with everyone who normally sat in the huddle. Captain Jack, Shrek, Tattoo, Hooch, Griff, everyone was already there. The PowerPoint was up, and the planning session began.

Major McMillan, the Brigade S2, briefed. A West Point grad—commonly called ring knockers—he was clean-shaven, thin, and lanky as a marathon runner. "UAVs show that the outpost isn't empty. Seems like Anti-Afghan Forces want to make it their new home."

"Men," Colonel Richardson, the droopy-faced Brigade commander, shouted. "That's my goddamn outpost, and I want it back."

"We believe that there is still time to do a quick insertion into the area," Major Dillinger, the Brigade ops officer, noted. "With the little bit of time we have, we believe that with the right air support and a team of special operators, we can take back the outpost."

"Sir, my Operational Detachment Alpha is at Bagram," Hooch

said. "The only SF members available are my Bravos. We won't have Afghan commandos with us."

"I don't give a shit about your Afghan commandos." Colonel Richardson jumped to his feet and approached the PowerPoint slide. "Your men are going to fast rope into this valley. My men at Abbottabad will set up a blocking force on this ridge line, killing anything attempting to flee."

"Sir, your men at Abbottabad are Provincial Reconstruction Team members," Hooch replied. "Civil affairs types."

"Today, everyone is infantry, damn it." Richardson was keen on making this operation come to life. "Captain Jack, I will need your men on this as well. I don't give a shit if you're JSOC either. You're operating in my AO, and if you don't like it, your team can get the hell out. I already informed your folks in Bagram. You're mine."

Captain Jack nodded. "Sir, you do realize that I only run a four-man shop, though, correct?"

"I wouldn't care if it was only a two-man shop." Colonel Richardson looked around the room with a grim expression. "Take Dr. Rex with you. He can be that one extra gun that may save your ass."

"Men," Major Dillinger said. His shaved head gleamed under the overhead lights. "We have three Apaches and one A-10 accessible for close air support. We can rebuild the outpost if we need. Use them freely; just make sure the Air Force TACPs have your call signs before you go out so there are no issues calling in close air support when you're on the ground."

"When do we leave?" Hooch asked.

"One hour," Colonel Richardson replied. "Men, I want to make myself very clear on this one. No one, and I mean no one, comes home until you have every one of my men accounted for. No one gets left behind. Do I make myself clear?"

The room stood in attention, and the colonel walked out the door. "Yes, sir," they replied, in unison.

Declan was concerned. No. More than that. He couldn't say anything to Rex. His friend needed to put on his game face. This was a high-risk operation, and there was no time to discuss it. "Walk with me," Colonel Davis told Declan, as if reading his mind. He took out a cigar. "You can't go on this one. I'm expecting casualties, and I can't afford to lose two of you."

"That's understood, sir." Declan looked at Colonel Davis. "Can I speak freely, sir?"

"We don't have a lot of time, but shoot."

"Sir, I played football as well, for a division-two school. I understand your analogy here but vehemently disagree. You're not in the fourth quarter of this fight. You're not even in the second half. You're still in the first half, and all they did is score against us."

"Is that so?" He knew he had the colonel's ear.

"Sir, I understand the importance of getting our men accounted for. And I agree we must get them back. But is this the way we do it? Do we use these types of limited assets?"

"What do you suggest?" Davis asked and puffed on his cigar.

"Sir, we just made contact this week with a major Afghan warlord willing to help us out. He has an entire army available at any waking moment. He's a legend here, if you will. I know this sounds crazy, but why don't we use him?"

"Use a warlord?"

"We can pay him to bring his network together, collect the intelligence we need to find our guys, and have him get them back for us. Taliban fear him, and it can work."

"Declan, if Colonel Richardson heard this conversation, he'd likely kick you off this base right now," Colonel Davis said. "He's adamant about this operation. What we are about to launch is going to happen, and there's nothing you or I can say to change his mind."

"I understand, sir."

"This is what I will tell you." Colonel Davis flicked his cigar, extinguishing the fire within. "You vet this so-called Afghan legend. Prove him to be everything you believe him to be. Then, and only then, will I consider your ideas of incorporating him into the security of this AO."

"Roger that, sir."

"Declan." Colonel Davis paused before the door of the TOC. "Although you're not going out on this particular mission, that doesn't mean you can't go out on future missions. I just want one of you two on this base at all times."

He walked back into the TOC, and Declan scooted himself back to his team room where Rex was likely getting ready. Declan's mind was moving a million miles an hour. He was concerned for Rex and the team about to head out, and he felt trapped being temporarily nailed to the FOB.

"You got everything you need?" he asked as he barged into the room.

"Yeah, man," Rex answered. He was wearing a gas mask. "How do I look?"

"Don't believe you'll need that stupid thing," Declan replied and opened the supply cabinet.

"What would the Afghans think if they saw us all wearing these, though?" Rex took off the mask. "Russians used gas, and that put some serious fear into the Afghans. I'm sure they didn't forget."

"Your outside-the-box thinking is brilliant, but I don't believe anyone would ever bite off on the ideas." Declan started loading some extra magazines as Rex inspected his kit. "I'm pissed I can't go out there with you guys."

"Don't worry, little buddy. You're better off." Rex started to insert some loaded magazines into his vest. "This is going to be a quick in and out. The odds are, we'll show up, Taliban will already be gone, and the bodies of the two GIs will be found inside the outpost."

"We'll see." Declan closed the closet.

"Six hours max. We go in, secure the site, conventional comes behind us, and takes it over. We leave. You sit back here, watching on the big screen, eating bonbons, sipping on some cherry cola, and enjoy the show."

Someone knocked on the door. Rex opened it, revealing two men. Declan didn't recognize them.

"Do you know where I can find a guy named Declan Collins?" the sandy-haired one asked. He was tall and good-looking in a frat-boy kind of way, with prominent cheekbones and a friendly smile.

"I'm right here." Declan looked at the man, trying to figure out who he was. "What can I help you with?"

"My name is TJ. Was wondering if you and I can link up tomorrow? Say around 1500?"

"Yeah, no problem. I'll be here." Declan was still confused. "What organization are you with?"

"OGA." He smiled again. "I'm looking forward to talking to you." Without another word, he stepped outside and closed the door behind him.

"Looks like you just made a new friend with one of those so called other government organizations," Rex said. "I gotta get going. Hold the fort while I'm gone."

"What the hell would OGA want from me?" Declan asked. "I've never heard of anything like this. Notice his accent? He wasn't American. Definitely wasn't with the CIA."

"He was a Brit, probably working for their Special Boat Service. They're doing a lot of counter drug ops alongside our DEA. Who knows, but I gotta go. See you on the flip side."

The room emptied. Declan was alone. His partner had walked out the door, possibly headed for the fight of his life. And now a twist had been thrown at him. Nothing was clear.

God, look out for my brothers. Help me understand the picture you presented. And, please, let Bran feel my love.

PART II

TWELVE

Declan, alone in his team room, sat quietly. His brother was headed out on a mission. Declan couldn't stop the scenarios from running through his head. He wanted to be with the guys, fighting the enemy, who had recently overrun an outpost. He wanted to be part of the search for the two GIs.

There was nothing for him to do. He could only sit back and watch from live feeds inside the TOC. He didn't want to watch them, especially if things went wrong. He needed an excuse to stay away from the TOC.

The next day, that excuse knocked on the door.

"Declan, can you accompany Jed and me tomorrow?" TJ appeared as Declan opened the door. He had a boxer's nose and carriage, but everything else about him was aristocratic. Declan had remembered who he was since the night before: TJ had sat in during one huddle meeting, and Declan had not seen him since. OGA teams rarely interacted with any military.

TJ was a team leader working counter narcotics for another government agency. It wasn't just any other government agency either. It was one of Great Britain's finest. In that OGA, he operated with a four-man team. Normally, they went out in teams of two. Tomorrow, they would need a third—Declan Collins.

"Yeah, no problem." He was eager; especially since OGA units didn't play by the same rules as the military. "When do you want to brief?"

"I'll pick you up and take you to the compound in about an hour," TJ continued. "We'll have some good chow and sit by the fire."

Sitting by the fire was code. Good Cuban cigars would be smoked, and firewater would be consumed. Luxuries like alcohol were forbidden in Afghanistan, especially around any US military. OGA wouldn't abuse their secret of forbidden consumptions, though, especially not the night before going out in the field. They were true professionals.

Time passed. TJ, Declan, and Jed were sitting poolside, watching the orange reflection of the fire shimmer off the water. The mingled scents of Johnnie Walker Red and puffs of cigar smoke filled the air.

"We're headed to Musharraf Village." TJ pulled out his map and pointed. "As you can tell, Musharraf sits in the middle of the AF/PAK border."

"Just the three of us?" Declan asked.

"And a handful of Afghan Border Police," TJ replied.

Pointing at the map, he continued with his brief. "This is the rat line used by the narcos. It either ends or begins with this village."

"We have a source," Jed said, and his freckled face broke into a grin. "Seems pretty reliable. Claims Musharraf is his village."

Declan was confused. "OK, an intel op. But why doesn't he just come to you guys?"

"We've been working this guy for months." Jed tapped the photo of the source in the dossier. "He's come through for us on more than one occasion. Always coming to us. Tomorrow, we need to go to him."

"I still don't get it, Brother."

"Declan," TJ said, speaking urgently. "We have a chance of procuring this entire village. And it's dead in the heart of Afghanistan's eastern narco rat line."

Declan knew that tomorrow could be a major win for TJ and Jed.

"Gents, I don't know about this one," he said. "A handful of ABP and three of us…"

"We can pull Brinkman if you can't go." The vein on TJ's temple pulsated.

"No you can't," Declan replied. "Brinkman is teamed with Clive. You guys never split teams. If something happened on this mission, and there were three of you on it, that would leave Clive to take over as a one-man shop."

"Exactly." TJ smiled, but his cheeks were still flushed. "The three of us sitting here know what would happen if three out of four of my team were taken out. It would be several weeks before London brought in a replacement team. And they would have to start everything from scratch."

"And we can't allow that," Jed replied while blowing smoke rings into the air from his Cohiba cigar.

"Half-a-day op. In and out and back to our compound. We leave at 0430. You in?"

"Hell yeah, I'm in." Declan looked over to TJ, who had calmed down considerably. "I won't even ask why you want me to come on board, though."

"If I told you it was as simple as just needing another body, you wouldn't believe me, now, would you?"

"Nope."

✟✟✟

The Toyota Hilux was fueled. Ammo rested in strategically positioned compartments hidden from plain sight. Border Police waited.

TJ, Jed, and Declan dressed in local garb—man-jammies and a good pair of sandals capable of running marathons if needed. Out of their office, headed to the staged vehicles, came an angel.

"Collins, this is Samina." Declan felt his eyes light up at the sight of this beautiful Afghan woman.

Samina's hand extended. "Nice to meet you, Declan."

"The pleasure is mine." He turned to TJ, wondering who she was.

"A King's grad," TJ explained. "Our best interpreter. Don't worry; she's one of our own. Not some twerp we found here in the Stan."

Samina's dark hair reminded him of Brannagh's. Seeing her brought back too many memories. He knew Bran was worried about his safety. Samina reminded him that he needed to make it home alive.

Jed, who was fist bumping everyone, was more than amped, ready for a fight like the scrapper he was. "Let's get this party started!"

The team loaded up inside the pickup. Jed was last in. With his AK-47 in one hand, he did a quick funky dance near the Hilux's front passenger door before getting in the vehicle. "Let's go!"

Declan felt the positive energy radiating from him. It was game time. He turned on his internal, sensory overdrive switch, and the team headed out.

THIRTEEN

After an hour or so, the village was now in sight. Declan had no clue whether they were still in Afghanistan, or if they had crossed into Pakistan. Either way, the team was on its own—no air or artillery cover, no military quick reaction team, just three operators, a female interpreter, and a handful of Afghan Border Police.

On one side of their truck were the Tora Bora Mountains, and on the other, was a steep drop-off. The only way to move was forward or backward. Declan knew that going back wasn't an option.

When they were still a few hundred yards away from the village, Jed's Afghan source met the team at a nearby rally point. With him were two of his local buddies. Hair on the back of Declan's neck began to rise as Jed got out of the vehicle to meet Sherz.

"Ah, my friend. You made it," Sherz greeted him as the rest of the team remained inside the Hilux. He was a short guy in his twenties with striking greenish-yellow cat eyes. His round face sported stubble that looked like a kid's attempt at playing grownup.

"C'mon, Brother. I told you we'd be here." Jed smiled, trying to reassure his source of the team's commitment. "This is your show, Brother, so what's the plan?"

"The elders want to meet you. They want to explain to you everything that's been going on here lately. They are not happy."

"Well, let's go, then." Declan could see that the little guy was eager to work this entire village.

"OK," Sherz began his instructions. "You come with us. Have your guys follow and park outside the wall next to us. We'll walk in from there. Tell ABP to stay a few hundred meters away, though. They are not trusted here."

"TJ, any reason Sherz's two buddies are toting around AKs?" Declan asked nervously.

"This is Afghanistan." TJ turned to face him in the back seat. "Everyone in the Stan has AKs."

Jed returned to his team after speaking with Sherz. He peeked inside the driver-side window and explained how the operation was to resume. Once he relayed the directions, he scooted back to his source.

As Jed went off, Samina said a quick prayer. Declan followed her lead.

"You two ready?" TJ asked.

"I guess we have no choice at this point," Declan replied.

"Remember, in and out," TJ reminded them. "No cowboys here. Everyone stick together. In and out."

Declan couldn't hold in his nervous laughter. "In and out, huh?"

"What's funny about that?" Samina asked.

"Nothing." Still laughing nervously, he explained. "Just reminds me of high school, listening to the Who."

"Who?"

Laughing, TJ tried explaining, "Samina, are you saying you've never heard of the Who?"

She was obviously confused by the musically driven joke, so TJ provided her with the insight. "SQUEEEEEZE-BOOOX baby! Are you saying you've never heard of the Who let alone 'Squeeze Box'?"

Declan didn't know if it was the joke or TJ's poor singing, but Samina found nothing funny about the ordeal. Reality was, this wasn't a funny time. Even under the worst of circumstances, though, guys like TJ and him always knew to get a in a quick laugh.

They parked their vehicles, and everyone began to exit. Villagers greeted Jed and TJ with open arms. The elders grabbed their shoulders and ushered them into the village. The mullah stood out with his henna-colored beard and black turban.

Something made him feel uneasy. He remembered what Spartacus taught him long ago. *There will be times when you feel something isn't right. There will be other times when you just know something isn't right. There is a difference between the two feelings. You'll know what I mean when you're in those situations.*

Declan knew something wasn't right. He reached back into the vehicle as if he had forgotten something, and then he made a quick phone call. "Mr. Haq, it's Declan."

"Declan, you sound like you're in trouble. Is everything all right?"

There was no time to speak. "Musharraf Village," Declan blurted out into the cell and then tapped the "end call" button.

With all his influence, Haq happened to be district governor where Musharraf Village rested. It was one of the most difficult districts to keep secure considering the magnitude of heroin being moved between it and Pakistan. A feared man, Haq was able to maintain relative peace in a district that even the military rarely explored.

Declan realized they were all in trouble. Within seconds of getting out of the vehicle, he smelled sourness in the air. No cooked goats; no Afghan flat bread, Naan; no roses that overwhelmed the senses, common during this time of year in Afghanistan.

"TJ, what's that smell?" He grabbed his counterpart's arm.

"Something isn't right, amigo."

Keeping his voice down, TJ responded. "Yeah, I know. This isn't good. Just stay cool. We gotta play it out."

Samina was already in interpreter mode, chattering away, translating the conversation in which Jed and the tribal elders were engaged. The two of them worked together as if they had done so forever.

Mr. Haq's enforcers were less than fifteen minutes out. That is, if Haq had understood Declan's message. There was no time to depend on Haq or any of his guys. The situation was sketchy at best.

The villagers, who at first appeared to be friendly, soon turned the tide. Obviously confused, they had no idea who Declan was. Overhearing Samina's translations, he immediately pulled out a business card.

"Here, I work for the *New York Times*." He handed the tribal elder an old business card from a journalist he had met only weeks earlier. It was an unethical tactic, but this was a life-or-death situation. Survival trumped ethics.

He knew Afghanistan's literacy rate was less than thirty-two percent. That meant the odds were in his favor that not one of them would be able to read the card.

"You see. These guys brought me along so I can tell the world about Afghanistan from an Afghan perspective and not just some typical, pro-American viewpoint."

He took out his digital camera and began taking pictures of the villagers, showing each one of them their image afterward. A move made in a desperate attempt to regain their trust.

Sherz immediately jumped into Declan's trap. "Wait, you work for the *New York Times*?"

"Yes, you may have read some of my columns." He tried reinforcing what appeared to be positive energy from Sherz.

Sherz had to be illiterate, though. He had probably never read an article in his life. The low literacy rate assisted Declan's odds on such a wager. After a moment, he seemed pleased that a journalist had come to their village. Declan was relieved he'd gotten away with it.

The team was bewildered. Even in their confusion, they played along, knowing things could get much worse if they didn't. Declan was on a roll. More important, he was buying time.

With his camera clicking, he continued playing the game of international journalist. He moved around the village, taking photos of clothes drying in the early Afghan summer sun, flat pans resting on open fires used to make Naan, and the people moving about the village. All of this could lead to some valuable intelligence if the team made it out alive. But his priority was no longer collecting intelligence. It was surviving.

FOURTEEN

D espite the Americans' forebodings, the villagers seemed happy. Declan continued his photo expedition, clicking away. Children had swarmed around him, asking to see their pictures displayed on his camera. From the corner of his eye, around one of the mud homes rested a red, four-door sedan. Jackpot!

He knew the car was something more than just a transport vehicle. The doors were open, and so was the trunk. Pieces of cut wire lay on the ground nearby. It was a VBIED in the making.

Violent Pashtu yells came in his direction.

He knew he had caused the commotion by getting too close to what was likely a weapon for the killing of coalition forces. He immediately pressed the delete button on his camera so no evidence would remain. A swarm of men ran toward him like killer African bees protecting their hive.

The angry men lifted him off the ground. He was soon floating in midair. Hands attempted to snatch his camera out of his hand.

"What are you doing?" he cried out as he lost control of any physical capabilities to flee.

Samina did her best to mediate the commotion. Just then, a village elder took off his sandal and slammed it into her head. Sandals worn in Afghanistan are unlike those in the west. They are made of rough, un-softened leather, sown by hand. They are much heavier than the synthetic ones found in modern locations, and their edges are not rounded, allowing the sides to easily cut into skin. Declan saw a stream of blood pour from the side of her face, below her ear.

"They're going to kill us," she screamed.

Declan heard vehicles approaching as clouds of smoke began to pick up. Haji Haq, son of Mr. Haq, appeared with a team of Muj fighters piled in two vehicles. They were only seconds away from Musharraf Village. *You guys couldn't come soon enough.*

Passing the lackadaisical and incompetent ABP standing by hundreds of yards away from the perimeter walls of Musharraf, Haji Haq and his team exfilled their vehicles, blazing into the village. A gunshot from the lead car fired near the entryway. It was Haji's signal to everyone that he was there.

Immediately, Declan felt the ground below his feet. For now, he had the power to tactically maneuver himself. Knowing where the entry of the compound was located, he darted away from the village hostiles.

"Let's go, let's go," TJ screamed. "Head toward the vehicles!"

The human shackles were unlocked. Haji stormed the place with total confidence, as if he and his army were leaders or assassins with the Taliban. TJ, Jed, Samina, and Declan flew past the villagers and headed toward Haji and his men. Temporarily stopping at Haji's side, Declan looked into his eyes. Before Declan could say anything, Haji gave one directive, "Go!"

Without thinking, Declan darted toward the vehicle like a gazelle chased by a lion. The others did the same. Gunshots rained toward the village center. As the sounds of lead passed Declan's ears, he realized a battle was unfolding.

"ABP, ABP!" He shouted directions to the others. "On foot, get to the ABP vehicles."

Samina flew toward the vehicles. Declan followed her lead. Next Jed, then TJ. Bullets ricocheted off the ground near their feet. As TJ and his team ran, more vehicles screeched to a stop at the entryway of the village.

Their Afghan Border Police counterparts joined the fight, firing their weapons into the village of narco-terrorists. ABP members shouted at Samina, reaching for her hand, attempting to pull her into their moving vehicle. Declan, TJ, and Jed were next in.

Bullets riddled the truck. The ABP tires were blown out, causing it to hit a rut, which broke the vehicle's axel. Haq's men stayed and fought while TJ's second Afghan team took up a defensive fighting position, swung around, and rescued the passengers.

As they stopped their pickup truck to get everyone into theirs, one of their members manning a Soviet RPK machine gun was shot in the chest. Jed picked up the slack and manned the RPK, trying to provide cover fire for Haji Haq and his men who had been stranded in the middle of the firefight.

"Go, go, go," TJ shouted at the driver.

"We can't leave them," Declan screamed.

"They're gone," TJ replied. "We gotta move before the rest of us get whacked. Move this vehicle now!"

TJ was right. Half of the ABP was gone, and there was no sign of any of Haq's men. Jed was still rocking and rolling the RPK towards the village, overloaded with adrenaline, shouting anything that came to mind. When the weapon was out of ammo, Jed continued squeezing the trigger.

"Is everyone OK?" TJ asked.

After checking himself, Declan realized a puddle of blood was congealing on the bed of the truck. "Someone's hit!"

"Who's hit?" TJ shouted.

"Shit! Samina! Samina!" Jed screamed.

Declan reached into a nearby med bag, grabbing bandages, gauze, and a packet of chitosan. Jed jumped off the RPK and rushed to her.

"Samina, where are you hit?" he asked. "You'll be OK. Just stay with us."

Samina was gurgling with every breath she took. Her breathing was getting more and more difficult.

"Give me a needle," Jed screamed.

Declan dug for a needle in the med bag while Jed and TJ did their best to patch up Samina's exit and entry wounds.

"I can't find one," he shouted. "I can't find a bloody needle! Where the hell are the needles?"

"Get out of the way," Jed ordered. "Give me the bag."

In the recent commotion, the med bag had unlocked itself. Supplies were scattered throughout the bed of the moving truck. Many of them were lost somewhere near the ground of the village outskirts.

"Collins, I need a needle ASAP," TJ said. "Got to regulate the pressure building up in Samina's lungs. If I don't get one, she's going to die."

Declan tried to ignore the pressure. He remembered what Spartacus had taught him and did his best to channel his emotions. After a few deep breaths, he continued the search.

Jed broke down, cradling Samina in his arms. "Don't go! Don't you leave me," he shouted into her eyes.

Declan didn't stop his search for a needle. TJ assisted, but to no avail. Samina's life was hanging now on hope and prayers alone. Jed broke down in tears holding her. TJ and Declan stood aside staring into her deep brown eyes as she gasped out gurgling breaths.

"Call Brinkman and Clive," TJ told him. "Call them and let them know we're en-route back to their location. We need the docs ready."

Declan reached Brinkman and passed on TJ's message. Immediately after he hung up, his phone rang.

It was Mr. Haq. "Declan, I have doctors ready. Get everyone to the district center."

"One of our own is down," he explained. "We need to get back to the compound ASAP, or she won't make it."

"My friend, Dr. James is here now," Haq calmly explained. "He will treat your guy first."

Dr. James was a member of Doctors Without Borders operating throughout all of eastern Afghanistan and Western Pakistan. He and Mr. Haq were longtime friends. Declan knew Dr. James well too, as he, like many NGOs, enjoyed Thursday escapades at the Haj. The doctor was exceptionally talented and had treated victims in the most hopeless conditions.

"TJ," Declan screamed over the blazing wind of the moving pickup truck. "Get us to the district center."

"No way!" Jed unleashed on Collins. "Screw you and your little Afghan pals! No way! We go back to the compound. Now!"

"Jed." TJ placed his hand on Jed's shoulder. "She won't make it that far."

The district center was less than a minute out. Even a minute might be too long. Samina needed medical assistance immediately. She was dying.

Pounding on the rear window of the driver's side, Jed pitched the change in plans, delivering a fragmentary order. "Head to the district center."

Mr. Haq stood outside, waiting with a handful of his men and Dr. James. What they were about to witness was rare.

Haq's son, Haji, was nowhere to be found, and Declan knew there could only be one reason for that. Haq's men began unloading bodies. Samina was first of the injured taken off.

Declan rushed over to Mr. Haq. "I'm sorry…" he began.

"No, Declan," he said. "I am sorry. We will do our best to take care of her."

Standing next to the vehicle, Jed began to vomit. His adrenaline was rapidly fleeing, his concern for Samina taking over.

"Mr. Haq, you saved us," TJ said.

"Mr. Haq, this is my buddy TJ."

"C'mon," Haq gestured to them.

They walked inside the district center's main office, and Haq offered them some bottled water. After taking a seat, TJ sat with his head hung low, hands shaking. Forgetting all cultural sensitivities, he looked up and asked, "Got any whiskey?"

Haq laughed. "Actually…"

He opened a cabinet drawer and pulled out a brand new bottle of expensive Johnnie Walker Blue Label. Declan and TJ looked at one another, dumbfounded, as he began pouring.

Mr. Haq raised his glass in gesture of a toast. "To good men lost and to those deserving to perish in hell."

All three took swigs of scotch.

As they were in mid gulps, Jed came through the doorway.

"What the hell is this?"

"Sit down, Brother," TJ said. "This is the guy who saved us. Mr. Haq."

"Yeah, whatever." Jed was in no mood for buddying up to some old Afghan warlord. "Anyone hear how Samina's doing?"

"Not yet, mate," TJ replied.

"I need to go check on her."

"Jed. Sit down." TJ needed to act like the leader he was. Years of operating in the UK's prestigious special boat service must have given him the tools to act with authority. "There's nothing we can do for her right now. Let Dr. James do his job. It's best that we stay out of his way."

Mr. Haq filled a glass for Jed. "Here."

"Thanks." He delivered an air toast in return. "Thank you, sir."

Silence took over. Few words could explain how anyone felt. Their lives had almost ended, and Samina's survival remained in question. Declan felt like an outsider in front of TJ and Jed. He wasn't a true member of their team, so he sat patiently, sipped his scotch, and wondered what would happen next.

"Do you men know what you did today?" Haq asked.

"Almost died," TJ muttered.

"Not funny, mate," Jed said. One of them could still lose her life.

"Men, you just brought a great amount of honor to my family. Haji was my son. My only son. He died like the warrior he was."

Haq didn't appear solemn. For the Muj, dying on the battlefield was an honor. His son had shown bravery facing certain death.

"I don't know what we could ever do to repay you for your loss," Declan tried his best at playing mediator.

"Declan, you and the coalition have already done so much for my Afghanistan. It's about time we begin to repay you."

"Get me my girl back," Jed whispered.

Haq chuckled. "Who? The one being operated on right now?"

"Yeah, Samina."

"She's Afghan," Haq said. "Muslim."

"No," Jed explained. "Samina is a Brit. Her family was from Afghanistan. Dad died fighting the Russians in the eighties. Her pregnant mother fled to London under political asylum. She's a Brit. Muslim? Yes. But a good one willing to live with her infidel. Me."

The tension in the room, already high, rose further.

"Do you love her?" Haq asked Jed. Haq was far from the typical Muj warlord. He was a level man.

"Planned on asking her to marry me when we got back to London in a couple of weeks."

Haq's glass had risen once again. "To the two of you. May you marry and have your own army of warriors one day."

For the first time in the past twenty-four hours, Declan knew they had obtained some degree of comfort. It wasn't Haq who comforted them. It was Samina.

She and Jed loved one another. His thoughts of her kept him strong. Every time Declan looked at her, he had thought of Brannagh. He knew TJ thought of his wife as well. Mr. Haq, well, he said he hoped he would be invited to the wedding so he could walk her down the aisle as her own father's replacement.

"I'll make a deal with the two of you," TJ said. "Samina lives, I will try getting a special visa for Mr. Haq to go to the UK."

Jed patiently waited for more. "Yeah?"

"If I can make that happen," TJ continued, "you have to allow Mr. Haq to walk her down the aisle."

Mr. Haq was more than excited, almost bursting out of the room to ensure Dr. James worked his magic to the fullest. Declan knew the conversation was all gibber. He also realized what TJ was doing was greatly needed to reduce some of the stress that filled the room.

"No, no, no…" TJ stopped Haq in his tracks. "The deal for you both is, not only will Mr. Haq have to walk her down the aisle, he also has to wear his black turban, man-jammies, and carry his AK. A shotgun wedding but Afghan style."

"This is the dumbest thing I ever heard of," Declan said. "Like you could ever get the visa let alone have the guy carry an AK at a wedding back home."

They consumed more booze as the twisted British humor slowly trickled to more serious thoughts.

Dr. James entered the office doorway covered with blood. He looked exhausted and far from the soap-opera doctor he usually resembled. All of them turned and looked at him. Declan felt his heart hammering in his chest.

"I need some water." He couldn't seem to stop sweating.

"How is she, Doc?" Declan asked.

Dr. James chugged his water, emptying the bottle. He turned his back on all the men and walked out of the room without saying a word.

"Doc," Jed screamed as he tried getting out of his chair.

TJ placed his hand on Jed's shoulder. "Let him go. He still has work to do."

Declan realized that Mr. Haq was true to his word. Declan had needed him today more than anything, and the old Pashtun warrior had come through and saved his life. Could trust with the Afghans be achieved? This question had been running through Declan's head.

FIFTEEN

In the mountainous region of northeast Pennsylvania, Brannagh had awakened several times in the middle of the night with terrible dreams. Dreams that Declan was in trouble. In one of them, he held an empty baby blanket, his face twisted in an expression of grief and horror. She was still anxious and in a fog when her parents arrived to help her with the house.

Although she hadn't expected them to show up so early, she tried to put on a good show.

"I just put on a pot of coffee," she told her mother. "You guys want some?"

"Sure. Dad is outside grabbing some tools." Brannagh knew she was using the opportunity to see how her daughter was holding up these days. "Have you heard from Declan lately?"

The question made Brannagh spill freshly brewed coffee on the saucer. "Last I heard, he was out on a mission."

Her mother stood behind her and placed her hands on Brannagh's shoulders. "He'll be all right."

"Of course he will." Brannagh turned and looked her mother in the eye. "Every time I speak to him..." She paused. "He just seems so happy being there."

"This is what he believes in," her mother said, "but is this what you believe in?"

"What's that supposed to mean?"

"You know," she continued. "Is this what you want? Do you want to be the spouse of a ghost, a man who is never home, a man who may never come home?"

Brannagh slammed the sugar spoon onto the table. "Don't start! Not today."

"Sweetie, I just want to make sure this is what you truly want," she said. "Is this the life that makes you happy?"

Her dad stood at the door, looking older than usual, looking angry. "Marie, why do you continuously bring up such rhetoric?"

"Rhetoric?" she asked. "You think it's healthy for our daughter to stay up all night worried sick about him?"

"She isn't alone," he answered. "Hundreds of thousands are in her exact position, worrying about the men and women over there."

"But he didn't have to go, Ardan. He isn't in the military."

Brannagh ran up the stairs, refusing to listen. In just a short while, she would have to face her own interrogation at her alma mater where she applied for a teaching position.

Once she was dressed, she headed back toward the stairs. The argument was more heated than when she had left.

"Don't you do this to her," her dad said. "She has enough stress with trying to get this 1890s farm house livable before he gets home. Stress trying to land her dream job. And surely she's stressed knowing her husband could be killed in Afghanistan."

"And while he's off playing GI Joe, we're the ones rebuilding this house."

"It's the least we can do…"

"Yeah?" she asked. "Well, who was there to help out your

brother?"

Her dad sounded furious, "Don't think for one second, that if Seamus had returned from Nam that my entire family wouldn't have supported him the way we're supporting Declan and Brannagh right now." Brannagh's eyes filled with tears.

"His death is what killed your father," she continued with her rant. Brannagh felt like screaming.

"And if Declan were to be killed, his mother and father would die inside," her dad added, "but he's not dead, and supporting him by fixing this house and comforting our daughter is our duty right now."

"He's not dying," Brannagh shouted and hurried down the stairs. "I have to go."

She walked out the door of her newly purchased, money-pit dream home. A home her husband might not ever see. Hurrying to her car, she felt tears stream down her cheeks. Key in the ignition, she slammed both hands on the steering wheel. *Declan, I need your strength.*

✝✝✝

"Mrs. Collins, thank you for joining us this morning." Principal Lowery introduced Brannagh to the rest of the interview board. A short, stubby man, he made up for it with wild floral ties. He was wearing one today, a Hawaiian print, along with a brown corduroy jacket that looked like something out of *Welcome Back, Kotter.*

"Thank you for the opportunity," she replied.

"You taught several years in New Jersey," Principal Lowery reminded the table. "Special Education, if I'm correct."

"That's correct," Brannagh said. "Five years, special education."

The interview continued for about twenty minutes, with questions from all three administrators. They asked the standard professional questions to ensure Brannagh was the right fit. Then they turned personal.

"Brannagh, your husband…" Vice Principal Montage began. In a white Polo shirt and blue blazer, he looked more like an athletic director than an administrator. He wore gray-tinted lenses that made it difficult for her to read his eyes. She tried to hide her discomfort.

"Declan." She paused. "My husband's name is Declan."

"Yes, Declan," Montage continued. "What does he do for a living?"

They had rehearsed this answer hundreds of times prior to his leaving for Afghanistan. "He works for the government. Currently he's away."

"Away?"

"Yes, in Afghanistan," Brannagh explained.

Superintendent Hlavack, a grandmotherly woman right down to the silver-gray bun, showed concern. "Mrs. Collins, how do you manage? I mean, how do you hold yourself up every day knowing he is over there?"

She paused, and then replied, "It's the greatest feeling in the world."

Completely dumbfounded by her response, Superintendent Hlavack demanded, "What do you mean?"

"Dr. Hlavack, my husband's a patriot. As his wife, I feel honored knowing he loves me and wants someone like me by his side."

Superintendent Hlavack seemed comfortable with her answer, but that didn't mean the rest of the board did.

"Mrs. Collins." Principal Lowery cleared his throat. "You must have days when it's extremely difficult being around others—especially young children."

"May I ask you a personal question?" Thinking about how Declan might handle this situation, Brannagh followed what she believed her husband would do. "When you come home from work, do you and your spouse ever fight?"

The principal appeared confused, but he played her game. "Of course there are times when we fight. That's part of a healthy marriage."

Brannagh smiled, knowing her fishing game had just landed her a large-mouth bass. "Who's to say fighting is healthy in a marriage? What scientific studies have been done to prove such a thing?"

Dr. Hlavack, a psychologist by trade, smiled. "That's interesting. Looking back, I've never run across any studies in my training."

"Ma'am, I believe there's a reason you haven't." Brannagh was reeling them in with each cast. Her hook was baited well. "My husband's not around. It's almost impossible for us to fight. He's in a war, and I'm thousands of miles away in northeast Pennsylvania. Really, what can we possibly fight over?"

The room was in shock, and Dr. Hlavack wouldn't allow an easy extra point after Brannagh's quick touchdown. "That still doesn't answer why you believe those studies fail to exist."

"Oh, I'm sorry." Brannagh was ready to kick her extra point. "Personally, I believe those studies don't exist because it's easier for people in miserable relationships to claim domestic fighting is healthy when in fact, there's nothing healthy about it at all."

"My dear, I believe many would argue with you on that one." Dr. Hlavack placed her chin on her folded hands and smiled.

"Yes, ma'am, I'm sure they would," Brannagh agreed. "But when they wake up every morning next to their spouse, that is if they're not sleeping in different rooms, do they immediately get butterflies thinking about how happy they are, knowing the love of their life is beside them like I do every morning?"

"But your spouse sleeps thousands of miles away from you," Vice Principal Montage pointed out.

"Sir, I assure you that he sleeps closer to me every evening while fighting in Afghanistan than the majority of spouses sleep physically next to one another on a nightly basis."

Dr. Hlavack looked directly into her eyes and smiled. "You truly are happy, aren't you?"

"Yes," Brannagh lied. "I would be much happier, though, if you told me I was hired." She sat patiently, waiting for whatever came next. Her hands were slick from what felt like a lifetime of perspiration.

"Brannagh, normally I would never do this," Dr. Hlavack explained, "but I don't believe we need to conduct any more interviews."

Shocked, Brannagh didn't know what to say, so she remained quiet.

"Would you all agree?" Dr. Hlavack looked around at her colleagues.

They all nodded.

"We'll have to check your references, of course," Dr. Hlavack said, "but I believe you're just the type of educator we've been searching for."

Brannagh was elated. She rushed out of the interview, hopped in her car, and then stopped everything.

I'm not ready to go back to the house.

Her cell phone rang. Not recognizing the odd number on the screen, she knew who it would be. "Hello? Is it really you?"

"Hey, babe." *Yes*, it was Declan on the other end.

"Declan! Oh my God!" Her morning was getting better moment by moment. "How are you? I miss you so much."

"I miss you too," he said. "It's been crazy around here lately."

"Tell me about it." Brannagh was all smiles. "I got the job."

"What? That's awesome!"

"Declan, do you know how awesome this really is?"

"Of course I do, baby," he assured her. "With how political education is these days and you having to know someone on the inside just to get an interview...wow!"

"I think attending Mountain Lake ever since I was a little girl might have had something to do with it," she told him.

"Who cares? The only thing that matters is that you got the job. It's not about how you got it, just that you did. You got it, Bran."

She stomped her feet and chanted with him. "I got it! Oh my goodness. Oh my goodness." She took a deep breath. "So tell me, how are you? How are you holding out?"

"Everything's good." His voice was flat.

No it wasn't. She could tell. "Declan, are you OK? Last night I dreamed that something went wrong."

"I'm fine," he said. "Everything's great. In fact, I was recently told that I'm wanted down in Texas to brief an incoming Army unit."

"What? Really? Does this mean I'll see you soon? How long will you be home?"

"One week. I'll be there late next Friday night. Then Sunday afternoon, I'll have to fly out to Texas."

"So we'll basically spend a day and a half together?" She wasn't too thrilled that it would be such a short visit.

Declan laughed. "You're like a bum. I give you a dime, and you want a dollar."

Brannagh didn't laugh. "No, honey. I just want you."

SIXTEEN

In spite of all he had been through, Declan was content. Speaking with Bran always brightened his mood. Finally, she had gotten the job she wanted. Sure, she was worried about him, but at least now she would have something else to occupy her mind. Something she loved.

"Hey, amigo." Rex entered the room. "How you feeling?"

"OK. Just got off the phone with Brannagh. She just got offered a teaching job."

"Nice," Rex said. "I'm happy for both of you. Are you OK?"

"I'm fine, Brother. Seriously."

"I hate doing this to you, but I need you to go out one last time before you take off."

Before he could explain any further, someone knocked on the team room door. Rex stormed toward the door like a Viking warrior ready for battle. Three members from JSOC entered.

"What's up, guys?" he asked.

Captain Jack, Tattoo, and Shrek entered the office.

"Heard about your little situation yesterday." Declan wondered who had told Captain Jack and his team about what had happened in Musharraf, but it could've been anybody. "You all right?"

Before Declan could say anything, Tattoo interrupted. "Damn right, he's all right."

Shrek wasn't as optimistic as Tattoo. "Hey, man, I'm sorry about yesterday. I heard that Samina made it through, if it makes you feel any better."

"I know. Thank God. And guys, seriously, I'm fine. You're here for a reason, though. What do you need?"

"Well," Rex chimed in, "That's what I wanted to talk to you about before they came here."

Looking up at Captain Jack, Declan asked, "Well?"

"Well..." Captain Jack approached the map posted on the wall and began his brief. "A Provincial Reconstruction Team, some Marine mentors to the Afghan National Army, and a handful of us are headed out tomorrow morning."

"And?" Declan asked.

"Rex said you were familiar with the area," Tattoo added. "We want you to come along."

"Why didn't Brigade let us know about this?"

"Dude, do you think Brigade has a clue about anything anymore?" Shrek replied. "All they care about is Kunar."

"And we all know how that's going for them," Rex added.

"Declan, I know yesterday was tough on you." Captain Jack went into officer mode. "If you need some time, I would completely understand."

"No." He needed this. "What's the deal?"

"See?" Rex looked at his JSOC buddies. "I told you this guy is unstoppable. That's my brother."

"First light, we head due east." Shrek scratched his beer gut through his 5.11 tan shirt. "A mass convoy moves out, doing a humanitarian aid operation in the Shinwari tribal district."

HUMRO missions were normally a walk in the park. Declan just didn't like the "mass convoy" part of the deal. "How many MRAPs are going to be used?"

"Four MRAPs and two up-armored HMMWVs," Captain Jack answered. "The Marine Embedded Training Team and their Afghan counterparts will be in two pickups."

"I hate MRAPs," Declan told them. "They're like moving coffins."

"That's why you're coming with us," Shrek said. "We go in our own vehicles."

Captain Jack concluded by explaining the details he and his team would be involved with. "We trail the convoy by a couple hundred yards with complete low vis."

"Low vis?" Declan laughed. "Following any convoy this far isn't really low vis."

"You want to go in an MRAP?" Tattoo asked.

"Low vis, it is," Declan agreed quickly. "But why are you guys going?"

Captain Jack was clearly pleased he had asked. "Actually, it's because of you."

"What?"

"Nobody has a clue about anything to do with the Shinwari Tribe," he explained. "We need for you to find out all you can about the so-called 'Lost tribe of the Israelites.' And while you do this, we'll serve as your added eyes and ears."

"The Shinwari Tribe? Fascinating people. Guys, I'm already in." The reasons still didn't make sense to him. "But really, why me?"

"You don't get it." Shrek tried his best. "None of us are trained in getting any understanding of these folks past kinetics."

"What's your overall objective?" Declan asked, feeling he might know where this was going.

"Rumor has it that, out of all the tribes, only the Mahmood has any liking towards the Shinwaris," Captain Jack explained.

"And you want to form an alliance?" Declan asked.

"An alliance?" Shrek shook his head. "No, we want to form a mass standing army between the two, in hopes they'll work together in an attempt to defeat the insurgency on the border."

Taking a line out of General Patton's famous speech, Declan muttered, "Let the other son of a bitch die for his country."

The light bulb in his head had finally come on. True counter insurgency would allow the locals to fight each other instead of them. Shrek and Tattoo patted him on the shoulder. He was part of their team now.

"Now you got it." Captain Jack shook his hand, and the JSOC members walked out the door.

SEVENTEEN

V ehicles stopped on top of a mountain ridge after hours of driving through steep switchbacks. US Army troops exfilled their MRAP and HMMWV vehicles, which overlooked numerous ridgelines. The small contingent of Marines and their Afghan National Army counterparts sped toward a fleeing sedan.

"Anyone know what the heck is going on?" Captain Jack asked his four-man team tucked behind the convoy in their low-visibility pickup.

"PRT is relaying that the suspected vehicle is likely a drug mover," Tattoo said from the backseat.

"I'm sinking us in to the rear of the convoy," Captain Jack said, clearly unnerved. "We don't need to be getting whacked from behind."

There was no sign of life near. The last village they passed had been miles away, deep inside one of the Tora Bora valleys. The movement only had a short distance left to travel before they reached their objective.

"AKs are firing from twelve o'clock," Declan said.

With the accelerator touching the floor, Captain Jack sped forward getting some cover from the rear MRAP. "Once we park, everyone get out and 360 around the vehicles. Overlook the drop-offs."

Shrek was already out of the pickup. "Collins, with me."

Shrek and Declan took the eastern flank while Captain Jack and Tattoo took the western one. "You have to be part mountain goat to get up this mountain side," Shrek told Declan.

"I'm convinced," he said, "Afghans are part mountain goat."

Just then, a message came across the radio. *Two males. One AK. Exfilled vehicle. Jumped westward down the cliff.*

"Damn," Shrek said. "If they made it, your description of Afghans being part mountain goat is pretty accurate."

After a quick search of the abandoned vehicle, they discovered five bags of freshly produced opium. The Marines showed the ANP how to disable the suspects' vehicle. One cigarette-sized pack of C4 detonated inside the engine block, ensuring no one could ever use the vehicle again.

"Ka-boom," Tattoo shouted. "I love that stuff."

"Hey, numb nuts," Captain Jack hollered at Tattoo. "Keep your eyes peeled."

After several minutes of pure quiet, Declan and his team were called to the front of the convoy.

"We're staging here, sir," the convoy team leader informed Captain Jack.

The team leader looked at his map and GPS. "Sir, if we follow this ridgeline down, we should fall right into the village."

"How many are you leaving behind with the vehicles?" Captain Jack asked.

"Two gunners each," the team leader explained. "We'll 360 the vehicles, leaving one gunner each to serve as our overwatch as we move down the mountain. The other gunners will secure the vehicles."

Tattoo, Declan, and Shrek all looked at Captain Jack and shook their heads in utter disbelief.

"We'll just have to deal with it," Captain Jack blurted.

The tactical movement was a complete gaggle. Tattoo took some control. "Collins, I'll take point. You cover my rear."

The three-man JSOC team, along with Declan, took the lead and headed down an old goat trail while the remainder forces followed. The trail led the team into a soup bowl. Mountainsides surrounded them as they positioned in the bottom of the range.

"What the hell are they doing?" Shrek asked in complete amazement.

With a small river running near their position, the Afghan National Army decided to cleanse themselves for daily prayer.

"This is a gaggle if I've ever seen one," Tattoo agreed. "Collins, help me get some bodies so we can set up 360 security."

"What the hell?" Captain Jack interjected. "Are we really going to allow these guys to take off their kits and start praying?"

"Sir, Marine 1 stated that this has been a constant issue they have been dealing with for months now," Shrek replied. "They can't control the ANP when it comes time for prayer. Guys have been shot over this crap."

"Keep your eyes peeled," Captain Jack told the entire twelve-man force positioned in the base of the mountains.

Though it seemed like hours, prayer only lasted a few minutes.

"Well, now that they prayed, they can do us a favor," Captain Jack said. "Send two men up that hillside and have them check out the caves. See if there's any sign of life up there." Captain Jack paced until news came back.

"Sir, they didn't see anything," the Marine reported.

"I don't like this." Captain Jack began scanning the horizon. "This is the perfect spot for us to get ambushed."

"Jack, we need to get out of here," Declan said.

Agreeing, the captain directed the team out of the soup bowl. "Go back the way we came," he instructed everyone. "My guys take rear security."

"Cover, cover, cover!" Directions filled the air.

A whistling sound screamed above Tattoo's and Declan's heads. Only milliseconds later, the RPG exploded in the center of the soup bowl.

"Cover fire," Tattoo ordered as he scanned through his sights for the enemy.

"Three o'clock," Declan shouted to him. "Four tangos moving your direction."

"Peel out," Captain Jack ordered. "What the heck?" He had just realized that half of his team had disappeared up the goat trail. He screamed toward them. "You bastards better give us some cover fire."

Declan and Tattoo rained bullets down on the enemy's last-known location. "Let me pop my head up," Tattoo shouted.

Declan sprayed his remaining rounds in the direction of the four insurgents' last-known location. "Reloading!"

Declan began reloading his M4, and Tattoo unleashed one round from his M203 grenade launcher.
"Take that, you assholes."

"Let's go, let's go," Declan urged him.

Captain Jack and Shrek were already halfway up the goat trail, taking up hasty fighting positions and unloading a barrage of rounds in the enemy's direction. Tattoo tapped Declan on the shoulder, signaling that he was moving out of the kill zone.

Once Tattoo fired his weapon nearby, Declan knew it was his turn. *Please, God, get me out of here in one piece.*

The opposing fire ceased.

"Keep going, keep going." Captain Jack directed him. The captain didn't want him to take up another hasty position, as the team was near the conventional guys with all of the heavy weapons mounted on their vehicles.

"Damn," Tattoo blurted as he reached the remaining three of them. "Nice seeing we had to fight our way out of there without any support."

"Those pukes will wish that incident never happened," Captain Jack said. "You three follow me."

Captain Jack marched his way over to Staff Sergeant O'Hara. O'Hara's men were chugging water, smoking, and joking.

"This isn't going to be good," Shrek said.

Grabbing Staff Sergeant O'Hara by his Kevlar vest, Captain Jack went off the deep end. "What was that? What the hell was that bullshit?"

"Sir…" Staff Sergeant O'Hara tried explaining the unexplainable.

"Don't you Sir me," Captain Jack shouted. "You cowards ran faster than the ANP!"

Not knowing to shut his mouth, O'Hara continued trying to explain himself. "Sir…"

"You piece of garbage. If it weren't for my guys and those four Marines providing cover fire, my men would be dead right now. "I'm taking over this cluster gaggle." Captain Jack's face was beat read.

"But, sir…"

"Shrek," Captain Jack ordered. "Get us the hell out of here."

"Roger that, sir," Shrek said. "Tattoo, Collins, take the lead. We go on foot until we reach the back-end drop-off. I only want drivers inside the vehicles. Everyone else, take the vehicles' flanks."

"Captain, if you don't mind, I ask that you drive our vehicle while the rest of us go on foot." Shrek clearly knew how to secure an area. Being in vehicular coffins meant too many dead spaces for sound visualizations of the area.

"I need to drive," Captain Jack said. "I need to calm down."

"Hey, sir, don't calm down too much," Shrek replied. "I need your eyes too."

"You got it." He gave him a fist bump, and the men moved out.

Declan was glad he was on foot and not trapped inside the truck. He appreciated the freedom of movement and the ability to breathe the mountain air. But more than being outside of the truck, he was relieved to still be alive.

EIGHTEEN

After a long day of fiascos, Declan couldn't be happier knowing he was back on the FOB. He hated the FOB but more so, he hated being stuck out with a bunch of troops who he believed had left his buddies out to dry.

"Would you believe that crap today?" he asked his JSOC counterparts. They took off their battle rattle in his shop.

Rex just started laughing. "So, good times in the Tora Bora, I see?"

"If you only knew," Shrek spouted.

"Let me get you combat heroes some freshly brewed two-day-old coffee."

"I like mine extra strong," Captain Jack said and unlaced his boots. Declan did the same, allowing his feet to breathe.

"Ah, like your women," Rex replied.

"Women." Declan finished a bottle of water and placed a healthy-sized dip of tobacco in his mouth.

"What about them?" Tattoo asked. "What? You got a hot date tonight or something?"

"Collins is going home in a couple of days, man," Rex replied.

"Nice." Shrek grinned. "How long are you goin' back for?"

"About a week and a half."

"Are you nuts?" Tattoo laughed. "It takes about two days to get to the states and about another two just to get back here."

"Man, that's a quick turn if I ever heard of one." Captain Jack swallowed his coffee. "It's almost not even worth the trip."

Looking at a wedding photo, Declan shook his head. "Seeing Brannagh for even one day is worth it."

"You're flying into the East Coast for a day or so, then turning straight to Texas to do a brief?" Captain Jack asked.

"Her best friend from Jersey is getting married," Declan tried explaining. "If I get home in time, we go to the wedding."

"Awesome," Tattoo said. "I love weddings. Free booze, music, dancing, pretty single women, love in the air. Weddings are the best."

"Who are you kidding?" Shrek said. "They only ask you to go to weddings for entertainment."

"What's that supposed to mean?" Tattoo asked.

"C'mon, everyone loves midgets at parties." Shrek unfolded the punch line. "Especially Filipino midgets."

"Fuck you!" Tattoo, the short Filipino, laughed with the others at his own expense.

"Dude, you just had two seriously rough days," Rex said. "Are you going to be OK at a wedding?"

"Who knows? This is what she wants, so this is what she'll get."

"You might be the craziest SOB I ever met," Rex said.

"If only you saw him today." Tattoo pretended to spray the room with an imaginary gun. "He was unloading rounds like he was Rambo or something."

The room busted out in jokes. Although Declan laughed with the team, he could only think about whether or not he actually would be ready to attend Brannagh's best friend's wedding. *If only she knew what I would do for her.*

NINETEEN

B rannagh shoved the argument with her mom to the back of her mind. She'd gotten the job she wanted, and more important, Declan was home. Although she knew he wasn't that excited about going to a wedding, she couldn't desert Lisa. Besides, doing normal things, going to normal places, made her life feel more settled than it had in a long time.

The wedding was held in Cape May in south Jersey, and Brannagh wore an off-the-shoulder dress in sea-foam green. She'd bought it because Declan had once said the color set off her eyes. Today he'd told her she looked nice, but he hadn't seemed to notice the dress or anything else about her. It was as if he was back, but he wasn't back. Not in his head. He'd explained it once as a light switch in his mind, and they both needed to figure out a way to flip that switch from off to on.

With his beard and sharp, prominent cheekbones, he looked older than his years, and even more handsome than she remembered. During the ceremony, she reached over to hold his hand. Something was wrong.

She felt no surge of energy between them, no connection. It was as if she were holding the hand of a stranger.

Brannagh looked over at him. She understood the beard, with its glint of red and tiny streaks of gray. He had grown it to blend in with the locals back in his other life. That didn't make her like it any more, though. Part of her wished he could just shave it and be like everyone else instead of looking like a freak of nature in the middle of summer.

They spoke little in the car on the way to the reception. Once they were there, mingling with the others in the Victorian gazebo, Brannagh was grateful that he took the glass of wine from a passing waiter. Maybe alcohol would loosen him up. Something he sure needed.

"It's beautiful here, isn't it?" She motioned to the ocean beyond the gazebo where they crowded with the rest of the guests.

"Chilly," he said. "You need your wrap?" He seemed eager to return to the car.

"No, I'm fine," she replied. His hazel eyes lacked their usual sparkle. They were softer, and *admit it*, she thought, sadder. "What about you?"

"Couldn't be better." The waiter passed by and Declan reached for another glass. He wasn't much of a drinker. Maybe he was trying to close the distance between them as well.

"Come on." She tugged on his arm. "I want to show you off to my friends."

"Can't we just talk?" he asked.

"Yes. That's what people do at these things."

Across the room, she spotted Daphne Wong and waved. Daph was easy to pick out in her short dress of tangerine silk. She met Brannagh's gaze with a smile and made her way through the crowd. A friendly face. That was what she needed to bring Declan out of his shell.

They hugged and Daph said, "You look beautiful. Who's the hot guy?"

That got a smile out of him.

"We met right before you left," Daph reminded him. "Brannagh and I taught together."

"That's right." There was no way she could tell if he remembered her or not.

"I almost didn't recognize you," Daph said. "We're happy you're back. Brannagh pretends she's tough, but we all know she misses you like crazy."

"I missed her too," he said, and sipped his wine.

"Well, we're proud of what you're doing." Daph patted his arm and grinned at Brannagh. "I'm going to check out the appetizers. Got to get something in my stomach, or I'll be as drunk as Slocum. Stay clear of him. He's blasted."

"Cameron Slocum?" Declan asked.

Brannagh nodded. "Our former principal. He's not a bad guy. He's just under a lot of pressure right now."

"And," Daph interrupted, "he gets drunk at the drop of a hat."

As if he'd heard his name—which was impossible in this crowd—a tall man with a shaved head turned from his conversation and looked directly at them.

"Too late," Brannagh said. "We've been spotted." That was the last thing Declan needed—a boring conversation with Dr. Sloshed.

"Here he comes," Daph whispered, "with snooty Carla. I hate to do it to you, but I've had enough of them for one night. I'm disappearing before he sees me."

In moments, Dr. Slocum and his wife joined them. As Brannagh made introductions, she could feel Declan pull away even more. It was wrong to insist they attend this wedding. No matter what her intentions were, she shouldn't have put him through it.

Daph had been right. Dr. Slocum was the scary, steady kind of drunk that made him appear indifferent. His watery blue eyes and measured speech gave him away, though. So did the helpless expression on his usually arrogant wife's face.

"I understand congratulations are in order," he said. "The job, I mean."

"Thank you. I think it'll be a good match."

"I know how passionate you are about special ed." He drained his glass and handed it to his wife as if she were a member of the wait staff. "Rest assured, my reference will be excellent."

Declan met her gaze as if to say he knew Slocum shouldn't be discussing anything about the job with her.

Slocum narrowed his eyes and studied Declan. "So what do you plan on doing when you come back for good?"

"Right now," Declan said, "my focus is on just that. Coming back."

"Indeed. And what then?"

"Well," he said, "I've always wanted to teach high school or college."

"Admirable." He glanced over at his wife and smiled. "Advanced degrees are in demand these days. A bachelor's won't cut it anymore."

"I know," Declan said.

"Well, good luck. Perhaps you can get some kind of education benefit from the government."

"Declan already has his master's," Brannagh said. She couldn't help herself.

"Oh, does he?" The doctor studied Declan for a moment. "You'd have to get rid of that beard. You don't want people to assume you converted and turned into an Al Qaeda terrorist."

Brannagh felt herself gasp.

"My beard? A terrorist?" Declan sounded incredulous. "Obviously, you don't know much history about world cultures. This is what the prophet Mohammad commanded among his followers."

"Are you pro Muslim? Did you convert?" Slocum's voice boomed, causing the guests close to them to turn and stare.

"Dr. Slocum!" Brannagh spat out the words. The reference be damned, no one was going to disrespect her husband, certainly not this officious drunk.

She started to tell him what she thought about him, but Declan reached out for her. His hand gripped hers, and she felt the connection. It was like a rock. Her rock, the rock she had missed. The light switch had been flipped.

"No, sir, not pro-Muslim. Just pro-culture."

Tears filled her eyes.

"Bran," Declan whispered.

She squeezed his hand tighter. "Let's go back to the room," she said.

TWENTY

A night of pure romance was exactly what Declan and Brannagh needed. It wasn't easy at first, but with love and time together, they embraced one another, entangling themselves with long-delayed passion. It was a short-lived yet passionate night of intimacy.

An hour-and-a-half car ride to Philadelphia International Airport felt like days for Declan. With the car parked at ticketing, he leaned over to his driver, placed one hand on Bran's cheek, and gave her a kiss.

"I love you."

Tears swelled in Bran's eyes. "I love you too."

"No need to cry, sweetie. This is what I was called to do."

Bran nodded in agreement, even though Declan knew she hated seeing him leave. Traveling light, he put one carry-on bag over his shoulder. He knew she was wondering if this would be the last time she would see her man. Declan didn't look back. He'd told her he loved her, and that was the most honest thing he knew.

"Where are you headed, sir?" the ticket agent asked.

"Fort Hood."

"How many bags?" she asked.

"One carry-on," he responded, still thinking of the expression on Bran's face.

Tickets in hand, going through security was a breeze. Declan needed to bite the dog that had bitten him the night before, so he headed to Chickie and Pete's for an early morning snack and brew.

"A bit early for one of those, isn't it?" one of the nearby patrons asked.

Collins didn't say a word. He wasn't in the talking mood. Instead he gestured to the Bloody Mary-drinking suit with a raised glass. The suit smiled, taking the gesture as an invitation to engage.

"Where you headed?"

"Fort Hood."

"I spent some years there back in the early sixties," the man said. "Some of the best years in my life."

"Really?" The guy seemed serious. "And why was that?"

"War," the suit replied. "It will either kill you or make you whole."

Declan nodded in tacit agreement and took a sip of Yuengling.

"You coming or going?"

"I guess you can say a bit of both," Declan told him.

In his beard, trekking boots, khaki pants, and Royal Robbins button-down, he probably looked the part to the suit next to him. It took one to know one.

"So who are you with?" Declan asked.

"Me? Oh, I'm not with anyone anymore," the suit said. "Used to be. That was years ago, though."

Declan's Crabbie Fries arrived.

"Looks good," the suit said. "I lost my taste for the Old Bay seasoning, though. I know a lot of folks feel bad for you guys, but not me."

"Is that so?" Declan was more interested in the cheese-drenched fries than he was in this Bloody Mary-swilling guy.

"That's right. Today's wars present many opportunities for guys like you. I can tell you're not some conventional military type. Special Forces? Intel? Contractor?"

Declan knew about foreign intel threats located all over the East Coast, and he wasn't ready to identify himself to a complete stranger.

"In your years of service, did you ever wonder who you actually truly were?" he asked the guy.

The suit smiled. "All the time, my friend."

"And how did you ever get over that confusion?"

"I realized I was a man, a husband, a father." He sipped more of the Bloody Mary. "A protector, a bank, a punching bag. I can go on, but I think you get my point."

"I think so."

Declan placed both hands around his bottle of beer, looking up at the flat screen. Local news covered some so-called religious group's protest of a local fallen soldier's funeral. He wondered whether his path in life was truly worth it any longer, considering the lack of respect among some Americans.

"Never forget one thing, son," the suit said. "This journey called life. You only get one chance at it. What you do for a living shouldn't make you who you are. What a man cherishes the most defines who he is."

Over the airport's loudspeaker, Declan heard the announcement for his flight. His plane was about to depart. After dropping a twenty on the bar, he grabbed his carry-on.

"Thanks for the advice."

"Good luck." The suit raised his glass. "Don't forget what I told you."

"No sir," he said. "I won't forget."

Declan left the bar and boarded his flight. In his seat, waiting for takeoff, he couldn't help but wonder who that man had been. Obviously, the suit was someone, someone with experience, someone special, but who? Declan felt his words of advice had mirrored words Spartacus had said over the years. He quietly listed to the things he cherished most: Brannagh, his buddies in arms, his sense of independence, his country, Brannagh...

TWENTY-ONE

D eclan enjoyed being around Ian and Brett. Both men were true out-of-the-box thinkers with years of special operations experience. They knew one another from brief interactions in eastern Afghanistan. Declan was the only one of the four not working within the Joint Improvised Explosive Device Defeat Organization contract. He was on a different contract, advising military leaders, but their missions were similar. Advisors were commonplace in Afghanistan.

"You know they're going to go in there and forget everything we just told them." Brett had been on this bit of theater before.

A former Delta Force operative, he was a clean-shaven redhead with pink skin covered in sun freckles.

"Happens every time," said Ian, a counter-IED specialist sporting a crew-cut.

"I don't get it," Declan said. "Why waste our time and a lot of taxpayer money taking us out of country just to do a quick debrief that everyone knows will do no one any good?"

"It's a shame too," Brett noted. "The younger troops, they won't forget. It's their leaders who will."

"Who cares about who remembers anything?" Ian shrugged. "You got to see your wives, at least, right?"

"No, I agree with Declan," Brett jumped in. "These trips waste a lot of people's time. I'm not doing these anymore. Leadership doesn't listen anyway."

"Gents, we have larger problems on our hands," Ian dropped an intel bomb on them. "Just got a report this morning that as soon as we get back, a major push on the Lagman-Serobi border will take place."

"Who's leading the push?" Brett asked.

Declan's mind began to churn. He knew the French had gotten massacred in that region not long ago. The area was completely controlled by the Taliban. This operation would likely end with serious bloodshed, and they all knew it.

"It's a major joint offensive," Ian continued. "SF, Brigade, Afghan Army, everyone's playing in this one. That's all I know. Hope you guys enjoyed the brief time with your wives."

"Not me," Brett said and pushed his red hair out of his eye. "I need a beer, a Lonestar. Leah said she wanted out. Can't take me being gone anymore."

Everyone put their glasses down. They never expected to see a career Delta guy's twenty-plus years of marriage come to a sudden halt. They were shocked.

"Leah's no dummy." Brett sighed. "Eight years at war and no end in sight. It's taken a toll on a lot of people."

Declan could only think about what life would be like if he didn't have Bran in his world. He was concerned about her worrying all the time. Thinking back to what the suit in the airport had told him, he was second guessing whether everything he was doing was worth it.

"You OK?" he asked.

"Nope." Brett replied and took the first swig from his bottle of beer. "I'm not OK. I was raised Irish Catholic just like you. Divorce is a word not found in my family's dictionary."

"What did you say to her?"

"I told her that I would ride this one out, and as soon as I got home, we would work on everything," Brett replied. "Only three months left, and I promised I wouldn't go back if that would keep us together."

"What did she say?" Declan asked.

Another round of drafts came to the bar. The men were brothers. Comforting Brett wasn't working, though. He was a seasoned operator, however, and knew how to let go of home problems once he set foot back in the Stan.

"She wouldn't listen." He looked down. "She's gone."

On the opposite end of the bar, Ian stood and muttered in disbelief, "No way."

"Yeah, man. She said that this was my life, and that I'd be miserable not being out with the guys fighting."

Declan didn't say much. He was still in shock. More so, he was confused, and concerned for Brett. "So are you really just going to ride this one out?"

"I don't have a choice, and it's killing me. I'm not just losing my wife. I'm losing my family. You don't have any kids. You can't understand what it's like."

"My wife had a miscarriage right before I left."

"Sorry, Dec," he said. "I didn't know. I've got twin boys, and I can't handle the thought of being just a weekend dad."

"What are you going to do?"

"I'm not getting any younger. I need to go back to school. Maybe start my own company or something."

"Doing what?" Declan asked.

"Same type of thing." Declan knew he had been thinking about this idea for some time. "Something in the defense contracting world. Start a company where I can still be involved but remain in the States."

Brett's vision made sense. He had been contracting himself out for many years, pocketing a lot of money. Starting his own company would be good for him. Quietly, Declan appreciated Brett's idea and hoped that if it came to fruition, he could one day be a part of it.

"Well, I'll make a deal with you, Brother," Ian said. "Start this company and I'll work for you."

Though everyone's attention was on Brett, his situational awareness had never left him. "Declan, you're quiet. Everything all right?"

"You know, when I flew out here two days ago, I met a man in the airport." He placed his elbows on the bar and remembered the suit. "He was one of our own. Older. More seasoned. Kind of like a founding father."

"He said something to you?" Brett asked. "He said something that you haven't been able to shake."

"Yeah."

Declan remembered the conversation clear as day. The past two nights, he'd fallen asleep reminiscing about what the suit had told him. He couldn't ignore his advice.

"This journey called life. You only get one chance at it. What you do for a living shouldn't make you who you are. What makes you who you are should be the things you cherish most."

"Bullocks," Ian cried. "That's the dumbest thing I ever heard."

"Really?" Declan asked. "Look around you. Look at Brett right now. Do you really think this war is what should determine the man he is?"

"Good advice," Brett cut in. "Listen, guys. Don't be like me, allowing this war to ruin your lives. Take care of your families. They need to come first."

"Brett, your life isn't ruined." Ian began throwing darts at the nearby board.

"Easier said, don't you think?" Declan muttered loud enough for the guys to hear.

"Fight the fight." Brett grabbed some darts out of Ian's hand and threw them one by one into the circles, landing the final dart in the bull's eye. "But when you're done fighting, go home, treat them like gold. Do your jobs, then go home and let someone else fill your shoes over there."

Declan listened intently. "Not enough guys like us exist, Brother. We're needed. It's a calling."

"No," Brett said. "A calling is meant for a teacher, a nurse, a priest, and what not. What we're doing isn't a calling. It's a life breaker."

"Life breakers and women takers." Ian turned and gawked at two college-age women who walked into the bar. "Hello, ladies."

The girls blew him off, and Declan laughed at his corny attempt. The conversation with Brett wasn't over, though.

"We're just going to have to agree to disagree, Brother," Declan replied. "What we're doing is no different than serving in uniform. That in itself is a calling."

Ian was getting out of control harassing the women. Declan was tired and knew a long flight awaited them in the morning. Texas to Atlanta, Atlanta to Dubai, then Dubai straight into Kabul. It was a flight no one enjoyed, especially hung-over.

"Speaking of calling," he told them. "I need to call the little lady, and then hit the rack."

Declan left the bar and headed to his room. It was late, so he decided to skip the call to Bran, knowing he'd speak with her first thing in the morning. He wanted some time alone to think about his own life, the life abroad, and the life with her.

PART III

TWENTY-TWO

T hirty-six hours had passed, and Declan was finally out of bed. His morning began as the sun was about to set. He believed sucking stale air throughout the sixteen-hour plane ride was what had put him down for a day and a half. But now he could breathe, and he was eager to get back into the game.

Declan loved seeing the snowcapped Tora Bora Mountains off in the distance. When he turned, he could also glimpse the Hindu Kush. Being surrounded by both mountain ranges pleased him to no end. They signaled his return.

Declan hurried, eager to get into his team room to link up with Rex. Once there, he saw Rex and his Fort Hood advisory counterparts along with Captain Jack, Tattoo, and Shrek from JSOC.

"Hey, sleeping beauty," Rex greeted him as he entered. "Feeling better?"

"I don't know what the heck hit me," Declan said, "but I felt like I got run over by an eighteen wheeler."

"Don't feel bad. We all got it." Brett's usually pink skin was pale and blotched with freckles.

"Well, glad to see you guys got your legs back." Rex was trying to take charge. "We're all headed out. Everyone. Mass offensive deep in the Uzbin Valley."

"Yeah, I already let them know, as soon as I found out." Ian was always on top of the mission tempo.

"I'm getting too old for this crap," Brett said under his breath, and Declan knew he was thinking about his failed marriage.

"We have rehearsals tonight, gents." Rex reached for the AK leaning against his desk, showing the men that their future operation would be one likely filled with extreme prejudice. "We need to rally with Third Group—1800 at their location."

"Are they taking the lead?" Captain Jack asked, hoping Third Group Special Forces would be running the show instead of leaving it to Brigade. Declan knew he still wasn't over the gaggle in the soup bowl.

"Unfortunately, no." Rex dropped the bombshell.

"Oh, what fun." Declan sighed.

"It's 1700. You all want to head over now?" Rex clearly rathered hang out with some of his old Special Forces teammates than stick around the office. "We can grab some chow at their compound real quick."

"Sounds like a plan," Captain Jack replied.

Declan walked beside his Viking warrior buddy and the other six, glad that it was calm for once. Without any of their battle rattle, the team straggled across the tarmac to Third Group's compound. Declan realized he'd forgotten his reflective belt, which, according to base policy, should be worn during hours of darkness. No one agreed with the policy, especially Captain Jack. Oh well. No one else was wearing one either.

As they started to pass the medical shop, a logistics First Sergeant stopped the team.

He glowered. "Where're your belts?"

"No time right now, Shirt." Captain Jack responded as the team continued walking.

"What do you mean, no time?" The sergeant wanted some action, and patrolling the mega base looking for non-compliers was likely all he got for eight months in country. "Where's your rank? You guys are out of uniform."

"What are you doing here?" After what they had been through, Captain Jack was in no mood for the garrison police. "With your brilliance, you should be a nuclear scientist."

The non-com's expression segued from predatory to perplexed. He couldn't do anything but stutter as Captain Jack continued his verbal assault. For the guys, it was better than any USO comedy tour.

"I'm an O-6," Jack told him. "Only one other man with me is in the military, and you don't need to know his rank or who he is. We messed up. We forgot our stupid belts because we're in a hurry, trying to win this godforsaken war while you stand here trying to fight a losing battle against one of your allies."

"But, sir."

"But, my ass." Captain Jack's fuse was short to say the least. "Now, we're going to our meeting, and you're going to walk away as if this never happened."

"Ah, ah, ah…"

"No need to say a word." After a step, Jack gave one last bit of advice. "Do yourself a favor. Next time you see guys with beards, wearing mix-and-match uniforms and trekking boots, look the other way."

Declan, like the rest of them, wanted to joke with Captain Jack afterwards, but he knew better. He hated seeing so many troops hanging around on the mega FOBs with nothing to do when a war was to be won.

"You know, we would all be better off in the Korengal or Pech River Valley with the boys, manning those outposts," Declan said. "We would be spared from the stupidity of this place."

"Actually, that sounds like a lot more fun than dealing with these yahoos." Rex kicked a stray soccer ball back to a local Afghan worker who was taking a break nearby. "After this operation, if I don't see anything happening for us, I may just request we go up to the Korengal for a couple of weeks. They could use our help."

"Let's talk about all that when we get done with this." Captain Jack pulled out his pass to enter the SOF compound.

Passing the Afghan guard who ensured only authorized persons entered Third Group's compound, Declan and the others met up with Hooch, Third Group's ODA commander.

"You guys are early." He looked surprised to see everyone at once. "Want to grab a bite before we go over tomorrow's CONOP?"

"Yes we do," Rex answered for everyone.

"Hooch, seriously, is this going to be as bad a gaggle as I think it will be?" Captain Jack furrowed his brow.

"You guessed it," Hooch replied. "Rumor has it that Brigade still doesn't have air cover approved for this thing."

"You have to be kidding me." Declan was as shocked as everyone else. "Aren't we supposed to head out early morning?"

"What is this crap?" Shrek asked as he took a bite of the meat before him.

"Goat," Hooch explained. "First chalk is scheduled for 0230," he said, referring to helicoptering in. "Seven chalks total. Bagram is having a difficult time coordinating air coverage because of some issues south of us in Paktia."

"So we may not even launch?" Ian asked.

"Colonel Roberts believes we're still launching as planned." Hooch looked skeptical. "We need to do our own CONOP with you guys and my men here in a bit. Once that's done, I'll tell Major Hemzai from ANA to get his guys ready for rehearsals—starting at 1900. We'll run his guys through a couple times, release everyone hopefully before 2100 if everything goes as planned, then link back here at 2330."

"Two and a half hours to cat nap, poop, shower, and kit up." Ian was as used to sleep deprivation as everyone else. "I love the Stan!"

Declan checked his watch, calculating what time it was back on the East Coast. He wanted to call Bran before he went out on this mission. No, he didn't just want to call her. He needed to. He'd done it from the start, so that if it was his last time saying *I love you*, she would at least have that.

Like a college football locker room, the SF team room was filled with some of the world's greatest athletes preparing to enter the arena as one champion team. Declan, who had never worn the Special Forces tab, was treated like one of their own.

"Hey, Brother," one of their intel sergeants shouted in Declan's direction. "You ready?"

"Yo, Griff!" Declan was pleased to see an old friend from previous missions. "Thought you went home on leave."

"And miss this?" Griff grinned. "I wouldn't miss this for the world."

"Well, it's nice seeing that we're on the same bird." Declan was relieved. Few worked as well as he and Griff.

"Nothing against you or anything," Griff said. "Just wish they'd let me go in on one of the lead chalks."

"Be careful what you ask for, Brother."

The CONOP was conducted. Declan hated how the military switched from an operations order to a concept of operations brief. Before going out, they ought to have precise details of a mission. The new

135

CONOP format was missing a lot, which caused confusion during enemy contact. He knew, though, that it'd be impossible to change the way the Army did things, whether he liked it or not.

TWENTY-THREE

The staging yard was packed with two dozen Special Forces operators and a small contingent of advisors. With them were about forty of their Afghan Commando counterparts. The darkness of night was no match for the vehicle's headlights, which lit the rehearsal grounds as if it were daytime.

"Everything seems locked in." Declan tugged on Rex's kit, ensuring nothing could fall off during the heat of battle. Inspecting one another was one of many golden rules followed prior to missions.

Rex turned off his night vision goggles. "I need some new batteries for my NVGs."

"Here." Declan reached into his kit bag. "I have plenty."

"Always prepared." He took the batteries from Declan, no doubt happy he wouldn't need to ask the supply sergeant for a favor. "You good?"

"Yeah." Declan closed up his bag. "Just didn't get the chance to call Brannagh. No big deal."

The Afghan commandos looked promising. Declan was impressed by the rehearsal, seeing them move with such precision. "Third Group's done a good job with these guys," he said and inspected his M-4.

Shrek came over to Rex and Declan with an expression of disbelief on his wide face. "This is such a cluster."

Declan had to laugh. To him, it appeared that few Americans serving in Afghanistan ever had anything good to say. Misery loves company, and he could feel a lot of misery in the air. Declan was grateful having Rex and his humor by his side.

"What do you mean?" Declan asked and felt himself smile.

"Major Hemzai just informed Hooch that some of his new guys weren't fast-rope certified." Shrek plopped down next to Captain Jack and Tattoo. "They need to come up with a solution real quick 'cause the choppers aren't going to touch ground for infil."

"Jack, you got your vehicle here?" Declan asked.

"Yeah."

Declan grabbed his kit and looked over at Rex. "Problem solved. Let's go."

Earlier in the day, Rex had been snooping around base for old equipment he could use for his famous workouts. Declan remembered him talking about some old rappelling ropes behind the logistics yard.

"Where are we going?" Captain Jack asked while they drove.

Rex punched Declan's shoulder. "If I'm hearing what this guy's saying, we're headed to the logistics yard."

"Those ropes aren't serviceable anymore." Shrek shook his head. "They'll never let us to use them."

"We're not asking." Declan laughed. "We're taking them."

The team was used to simply procuring equipment without asking. Declan knew how Big Army was with paperwork, and he remembered hearing Rex's horror stories from when he was a Captain in SF.

"Park here." Rex pointed to a discreet location behind two conex boxes. "Jack, keep it running. Everyone else, come with me."

The men skillfully moved through the yard, using shadows as their concealment. Their every movement was precise, as if they were sneaking into a village to kidnap someone. Instead of a person, though, they were about to kidnap an unserviceable fast rope.

"Damn, these things are heavy," Shrek blurted as the team moved the rope toward the vehicle.

"It's in." Rex chuckled, no longer seeming concerned. "Let's go."

The team sped off with the vehicle's lights turned off for several yards. Once they cleared, Captain Jack turned the lights on as if nothing had happened.

When they returned to the rehearsal yard, they saw the SF team was just sitting around.

"This doesn't look good," Jack said to Hooch, the SF team leader. "What's going on?"

"Brigade is contemplating canning the op because some of the commandos aren't fast-rope certified." Hooch looked in the bed of Jack's pickup.

"Problem solved," Declan announced. "We got the rope. Let's hook it to the tower and get them certified right away."

"Where the hell did you guys get this?" Hooch shook his head in disbelief. "Never mind. I don't want to know."

Declan felt good. He had just contributed to the mission. No matter how small or large, he believed it was a worthy contribution. If they took care of minor details, they wouldn't have to worry about the big things as the bigger things would just come together naturally.

"Major Hemzai, we're getting your men certified." Hooch pointed at the rope.

"No sleep tonight." Shrek sat against a nearby wall and placed his kit bag behind his head.

Griff walked over to Declan, shaking his head. "I don't know how you guys did it, but I need to get out of the Army and come work for you all."

Sitting next to Declan, Brett looked up at Griff with a rare grin. "I thought you were going back to Cajun Country to try out for Discovery Channel's *Swamp Wars*."

"Whatever." Griff didn't take offense. He was used to being picked on for his backwoods Cajun antics.

Rex glanced down at his watch. "0200, thirty minutes to launch. Does anyone know whether or not we're even going?"

Seconds passed, and Hooch's dark silhouette appeared as he stood in the back of one of SOF's HMMWVs.

He shouted to the crowd of operators. "Roxanne! Roxanne, men!"

That was the code word, giving them the green light to go on their offensive. Declan cheered along with everyone else, even chiming in to sing the famous Police song, "Roxanne." Music soothed the beast, he thought.

As excited as he was, an anxious tension began to set in. "Rex, you're on chalk three, right?"

"Yup," Rex replied while gathering his gear. "You ready?"

"Ready as I'll ever be." He took a deep breath to calm his nerves.

"The area will already be cleared by the time you and Griff come in." Rex met Declan's gaze, looking like a big brother. "I'll already be on the ground waiting for you."

Overhearing their conversation, Griff said, "Dude, we got the easy job."

Declan didn't respond. He looked over at his flying partner and waited for more.

"We hit up the village elders." Griff jerked on his kit bag's pull tabs. "I grab the kinetic intel. You grab the atmospherics."

Declan nodded. "Too easy."

Everyone started walking over to the helo pad. Declan threw all his personal items, which included a photo of Brannagh, in Captain Jack's vehicle. He looked at her image one last time before the mission, and thought, *I love you, baby*.

TWENTY-FOUR

B rannagh was glad that Caitlin and Joe were over for the weekend to help out with the rebuilding of the house. She needed the company. She loved her sister and brother-in-law, and their happiness was contagious, especially now that they had a baby on the way.

Crickets chirped in the summer night. Infomercials reeled on the master bedroom's television, which Brannagh had accidently left on prior to falling asleep. Caitlin and Joe slept peacefully in the guest room.

Brannagh startled Apoc, her American bulldog, as she hopped out of bed. Something wasn't right, she thought. Apoc jumped off the bed, running down the stairs and barking at the door as if an intruder were there.

Brannagh let him outside for a midnight potty break. Sipping on a cool glass of water, she couldn't shake her nightmare. She ran her finger over the magnetized wedding photo on the refrigerator. *When you get home, I'm going to fall in love with you all over again.*

"Sweetie, you okay?" Caitlin asked as she entered the kitchen.

"Couldn't sleep." Brannagh replied, not bothering to hide the fact that she'd been looking at Declan's photo.

"He's an amazing man," Caitlin said.

"I know."

They walked outside, took seats on two Victorian rocking chairs, and stared into the star-bright night. The late hour was peaceful, the faint noise of the wilderness serving as the backdrop for their conversation.

"It's so serene out here," Caitlin said. "Did you see that star? Make a wish."

"I already did." Brannagh petted Apoc. "You know what I wished for, though."

"Of course." Caitlin grabbed her hand.

"I wish he hadn't come home a couple of weeks ago." She sipped more water.

"What? What do you mean?"

"I had to start all over again," she said. "Don't get me wrong, I miss him terribly, but seeing him for such a short period only to have him leave so suddenly—I just don't think it was worth it."

"I don't know how you did it." Caitlin placed her hand on hers. "I couldn't."

"Sure you could," Brannagh told her. "It's a war. We all do what we have to do. That means them over there, and us over here. It's that simple and that complicated."

"At least he got to escort you to the wedding, and he was here when you landed the job. I'm sure that was important to him."

Brannagh hid a grin from her sister. This probably wasn't the time to tell her about how Declan put her former principal, Cameron Slocum, in his place at the wedding.

"I'm sure it was. It was to me."

"He had to go, didn't he?" Caitlin leaned back and placed her hands on her head.

Brannagh paused, remembering why Declan had decided to go abroad. She couldn't be more proud.

"Yeah." She took a deep breath. "You know, he never applied for this job."

"What?" Caitlin gasped. "What do you mean?"

"He was recruited."

"Recruited? By whom?"

"I don't know. He never told me."

"Are you crazy?" She perched on the edge of the chair like a schoolgirl. "You don't even know who he's working for?"

"Obviously it's the government." Her sister really didn't have a clue. "It's not like he's working for the mafia."

"Yeah right." Joe overheard the conversation as he walked out the door. "This government's worse than the mafia."

"Shut up, Joe." Caitlin looked at her husband with wide eyes. "Don't start with your anti-government rant, you big hippie."

He grinned. "What? I'm just saying."

Bran grew tired. She was tired of being awake in the middle of the night and tired of hearing Joe's diatribes. It was time to go back to her room to find safe refuge away from Joe. She knew she was already awake for the day, but she needed to get out of there.

"It's way too early in the morning to have this conversation." She got out of her seat and headed back inside.

"Bran." Caitlin sipped her glass of water. "You sure you're okay?"

"I don't know. I just have a weird feeling right now." She turned around, knowing she wouldn't be able to go back to sleep.

"What?" Joe began rough housing with Apoc. "You think something happened to him?"

"No." She put an end to the idea immediately. "I would have

known if it were anything like that."

"When's the last time you heard from him?" Joe asked.

"A few days ago. He'd been traveling and wasn't feeling well."

"See, you have nothing to worry about then." Caitlin tried pushing Apoc off her husband. "He isn't out on any mission if he wasn't feeling well."

Brannagh grabbed Apoc by the collar, keeping him away from Joe. "You don't know Declan and other guys like him. They don't get sick, and when they do, it doesn't keep them out of the game very long."

"Yeah, but doesn't he call you before he goes out?" Joe asked.

"He tries to. But he's not the type to call me if he knows I'm sleeping."

"Sweetie, can you get me some more?" Caitlin finished her glass of water and handed it to Joe. "That's the dumbest thing I ever heard." She looked back to Brannagh. "He really won't call you if he thinks you might be sleeping? Doesn't he realize you would be overjoyed to hear from him any time, day or night?"

"No, he gets that." Brannagh settled into the chair again. "When he's home, he has a difficult time getting me out of bed for work. He says I look like an angel when I sleep and it's too difficult for him to wake me." *Sleeping angel* was what he called her, but she couldn't share that, even with her sister.

"He's the total package, Bran," Caitlin gushed. "He's brilliant. He's romantic. And he's a warrior who can protect you no matter what. I'm so happy he's my brother-in-law."

Brannagh looked around the moonlit field in front of her then stared up into the stars twinkling high above. She had always felt comforted believing each star represented someone she knew who had passed and was looking down on her. She didn't want her husband to be one of those stars.

She grabbed Caitlin's hand. "I just hope he comes home soon. He has to."

TWENTY-FIVE

A swarm of helicopters hovered over the tarmac. Chalks one and two were already on their way to seize the initiative. Rex, already seated in his Chinook with the remainder of chalk three, looked out of the back, giving Declan a thumbs up as the chalk taxied away from its pad.

A small force of some of America's best warriors was about to take the fight to the enemy. While the nerves had fully set in Declan's body, he was eager to join them.

He turned to Griff. "Ready to load up?"

"Don't get too excited." Griff adjusted some of his ammunition magazines. "We got about a half-hour."

The three chalks, packed with special operators, Afghan commandos, and a handful of advisors, would engage the enemy in about twenty minutes. Declan knew early morning raids occurring in hours of darkness often caused serious blowback among the locals. He had his game face on, yet he realized there was time to spare. He pulled out a book.

"It may be a bit too late for that, amigo," Griff said.

"Not praying," Declan replied while skimming through the text. "It's the Koran."

"Oh great," Griff barked. "Tell me you didn't convert to Islam."

"Are you kidding me? My family would kill me. Did I ever tell you that my mom was once in the convent?"

"So what the heck are you doing with that then?"

"Transforming myself." Declan turned on his headlamp and began reading some suras.

"You think you're some kind of Afghan avatar or something?" Griff asked. "You can't transform yourself."

"Au contraire, mon frère," Declan replied. "We transform ourselves every day. Every person we interact with initiates some mild form of transformation. In this line of work, it's critical to be able to transform yourself if you ever plan on being successful. You really want to get out of the military as you said earlier?"

"Yeah, man, I do."

"Well, you better start learning how critical transformation is," Declan said. "It's a skill, a critical skill that will keep you alive."

"Yeah, but what you're doing, isn't that kind of catering to the enemy?" Griff scratched at his beard.

"Quite the opposite." Declan closed the Koran. "One of the first rules of infiltration and elicitation techniques is what?"

Griff shrugged. "Depends, I guess, on who you're dealing with."

"No, it doesn't," Declan explained while returning his Koran to his kit bag. "One of the first rules in elicitation or infiltration is ensuring those you're trying to work know that you're the real deal, the man. Someone not to screw with, and someone with intelligence and full understanding of their culture."

"Makes sense." Griff agreed and placed a heaping glob of Copenhagen dip into his mouth.

"No, you still don't get it." Declan said. "None of this means you need to come across as a complete jerk or some type of tough guy. It means that your strength must come from your mind. Know what gets your sources hot, cold, warm, and uncomfortable—you get the point."

"Yeah, I get it, but how will the Koran do that?" Griff spat on the ground.

"Afghanistan is an Islamic country." Declan placed his can of Skoal back in his pocket. "Ever read the Koran to a bunch of Muslims who can't read themselves?"

"Thirty-two percent literacy rate." Griff was finally understanding. "Play the role of the mullah."

"You're only partially there, Brother." Declan took a seat near the helo to get a last-second inspection. "Turn the people on the mullahs. You and I both know that the majority of the village mullahs are on the Taliban side. Educate the villagers on our truths about Islam."

"Brilliant." Griff clapped his hands together. "So you want to teach the villagers everything nice about Islam whether it be accurate or not."

"That's where you failed to understand," Declan told him. "Islam is an Abrahamic religion. Agree to disagree, but reality is, just like Christianity and Judaism, no one can be too certain about accuracies. That's where faith comes into play."

"Man, my Southern Baptist mama would put a cross to your face if she ever heard you say that."

Declan chuckled. "It's not about right or wrong. It's about belief and faith. You can't have either unless you have the tools needed to bring about both."

"And we need to provide them with the tools?" Griff asked with a bit of hesitation.

"Religion can be a great influence," he replied. "It's started many wars, my friend. Let's try using it to end today's battle."

✝✝✝

A team of helo crewmembers exited Declan and Griff's bird. They were about to conduct one last outside inspection. The door gunner waved for the men to begin loading themselves into the chopper.

The chatter on Griff's SATCOM radio grew louder. Explosions and voices shouting directions were broadcast in a cloud of static. Declan got quiet and tried to listen in.

"What's going on?" he asked Griff.

"They made it to the objective. Sounds like Taliban were tipped off somehow."

"Let's go," The helicopter's crew chief shouted to them as the props were in full rotation, kicking sand up into the air.

Hurrying into the fully loaded humanitarian-aid Black Hawk, both harnessed themselves into the left-hand side with feet dangling on the bird's skids. It was go time.

"Let's do this," Declan shouted over to Griff.

They bumped fists, and the helo took off. Declan eagerly awaited linking up with the rest of the operators. Earpieces and throat mics were being used, but they were too far out to transmit. Declan could only hear the commotion on the ground.

"Sounds like they saved us some fun after all," Griff shouted while positioning his weapon at the ready.

They were less than two minutes out from the landing zone now. The radio chatter intensified. Bullets could be heard in the background of every transmission. An infrared beacon appeared as Declan's bird approached the landing zone. His heart raced.

"Raven 2, this is Raven 1."

Declan braced himself for landing. It was Rex calling. "Go ahead, Raven 1."

"It's going to be a hot landing."

"Roger that." Declan answered with sweat beading in his palms. *Dear God, if you're listening, give me strength and courage.*

"RPG! Three o'clock!" Griff shouted as he and the door gunner unloaded rounds of hell toward the terrorists. The pilot swiftly maneuvered, forcing any return fire to cease.

Griff lost his balance as the pilots initiated evasive maneuvers. Without hesitation, Declan grabbed the back of his partner's ammo vest. The men quickly became disoriented reaching for anything they could get their hands on to secure themselves.

The helo banked hard in the direction of the RPG fire. Declan grabbed the door handle with one hand while managing to hold his weapon firmly with the other. The defensive move by the pilot wasn't enough.

"We're hit! We're hit!" the pilot shouted while trying to maintain what little control he had over the Black Hawk. "We're going down."

Holy crap! Out of nowhere, the once-flying Black Hawk had sunk deep into a wheat field. It was caught in the middle of insurgents on one side and American forces on the other.

"Dude, you good?" Griff asked Declan.

"I'm good," he shouted over the still spinning rotors. "I can't feel my arms."

"Can you feel your legs?" Griff didn't seem too concerned. His adrenaline was in overdrive.

"Yeah."

"Cover me." Griff jumped off the helo and immediately circled to the opposite side in an attempt to take cover once he realized the rotor had stopped spinning.

"Whiskey 1, stay put. We're headed toward you." Hooch's voice sounded over the radio.

Bullets from Taliban fighters hit the helo. It was too close for comfort.

"Cover me," Declan told Griff through his throat mic. He took a few deep breaths followed by one simple directive. "Look behind you."

A wave of twelve men rushed toward the downed helo. A few paces into it, the two teams of four would hit the deck while the four covering would bounce up to continue the process of keeping the insurgents' heads down with their fire.

Captain Jack, Rex, Tattoo, and Brett were in the middle formation and linked up with Declan and Griff first.

"You guys all right?" Captain Jack asked while sucking wind.

"We're good." Griff maintained aim in the direction of the insurgents' last-known location. "Collins can't feel his arms."

"I'm all right," Declan shouted while firing in the direction of a black silhouette. "Just some pins and needles now."

"Sending one to your location," Tattoo transmitted over the net.

"Dude, I told you I'm fine," Declan shouted.

"Not you." Tattoo tucked himself closer to the helo. "The gunner's face is bashed. He must have done it when you landed."

"Link them up with the doc." Captain Jack directed Rex and Brett to take the crew back to their original location near a small creek on the outskirts of the village. "The rest of us need to secure this bird so we can get ANA over here to grab what they can and take it over to the rally point."

The sun began to rise over the horizon. NVGs were no longer useful. Vision was poor due to the mass amounts of fog and smoke lingering from expenditures fired earlier. Declan hoped the peace of morning and not having had to fire in the past twenty minutes were good signs.

After a quick inspection of the bird, he looked to Captain Jack. "Everything's off loaded."

"OK." Jack directed the remaining men, "Let's head back to the rally point."

A team of Afghan commandos stayed behind, taking up security around the downed helo. Enemy contact was null for some time. Declan hoped that, by now, the area was fully secured, but something in the back of his head told him otherwise.

Rex walked over to grab the security team. "Perimeter is secured. The blocking force is taking a beating, though."

"Our guys?" Tattoo asked.

"No," Rex explained while helping Tattoo to his feet. "The French over the ridge in Serobi. Tangos met our conventional guys, and they took a hard turn west into Serobi. I guess it caught the French off guard."

Captain Jack recognized his pain. "You still hurting?"

"Yeah, having a hard time turning my neck," Declan said. "Can't shake these damn pins and needles."

"You need to see the doc," Rex said.

"Let us finish the op, and I promise once we get back to the FOB, I'll see the doc." Declan didn't want to be the weak one of the bunch.

"All right." Rex understood his concerns. "We finish this, get home, and you go right to the med tent."

"You got it, boss."

It was time to link up with Hooch and the rest of the SOF team and begin collecting intelligence. Declan knew that it was his time to shine. The only reason he was even brought on this mission was because Hooch knew he knew how to work the locals. Pain or not, he couldn't let him down.

TWENTY-SIX

T he area was secured. Four terrorists were captured. Six more were killed. With one broken Black Hawk grounded and locals in complete shock, Declan knew the mission wasn't over. Atmospherics were desperately needed, and that was his job.

"They had all the village elders gather in the courtyard." Rex pointed his finger in the direction of several gray-bearded Afghan villagers. "They're not happy."

"Would you be happy?" Declan grimaced in pain as he turned his head trying to look at his counterpart.

Rex cocked his head, as if he realized that Declan's neck wasn't right. "You sure you're OK?"

Walking toward the villagers, Declan failed to respond. He was on a mission. Griff was already in interrogator mode, trying to actively elicit information from the villagers. Declan knew this was not the time for continued hostility. He needed to be the good cop.

"Salam Alaikum," he greeted the tribal elders.

One red-bearded elder stood out. He was the instigator of the bunch, and he continued with his Pashtun rant. Declan needed to be cool yet show the small contingent of elders that none of them was in control over the situation. He needed to show them that he was.

"Translate every word I say," he told Awarang, his interpreter. "Don't interpret me. I want strict translations."

"Yes, sir."

"We came here today in peace. This is why your children now have pens, paper, and soccer balls." While introducing his speech, Declan opened his Arabic-English Koran. "Every one of you broke your religious obligations to respect and treat the people of the book with kindness. Instead, your sons shot at us, trying to kill us."

"He wants you to know the men who shot at you weren't part of the village." Awarang pointed at the tribal leader.

"Taliban were here in the early morning." Declan held up a seized AK-47.

Still, the elders attempted to portray themselves as the peace-loving types. Declan's translator began to laugh. "They continue to insist that the men who shot at us weren't part of the village."

"Taqiyyah won't work with me. I know Islam. The Prophet Mohammed, may peace be upon him, specifically states 'Truly Allah guides not one who transgresses and lies.' But you just lied to me." Declan pointed to sura 40:28 so the elders would see that he knew the very religion that they lived their lives by.

Their spiritual leader, the mullah, refused to look at him. He was quiet. Declan knew this was a sign, so he pointed to another passage in his Koran. "Read this."

"He says he can't read English."

"Read the Arabic, then," Declan shouted.

"Declan, he says he can't read Arabic either."

Village elders looked perplexed. They couldn't believe that their own mullah could not read the Koran in Arabic. They were more amazed that their own mullah couldn't read in Pashtun either. The trap was set, and the lion had placed his foot in it.

Declan knew he had just caught the predator.

"You listen to this fake religious leader?" He pointed to the mullah. "How can he be a mullah if he cannot read the Koran in Arabic?"

The elders looked startled. None of them could read, but their faith rested in their mullah. He knew the elders felt betrayed by one of their own. Now he needed to squash any village punishment that would likely come against the mullah for his years of lies.

"The Koran states, 'My Lord! Forgive and have mercy, for thou art best of all who show mercy.'" Declan began reading aloud from the many suras regarding forgiveness he had previously highlighted.

Awarang stopped and turned to him. "They want to know if you're an American mullah."

"Tell them that I am a student."

Within five minutes of speaking with the village elders, Declan settled the hostilities. One elder ordered chai and Naan to be served. Poison was Declan's first thought, but after the elders consumed the early afternoon treat, he joined them.

"Many Afghans I meet claim they are Pashtun before claiming to be Muslim," he said, and sipped on his chai.

The tribal chief spoke, and Awarang translated. "This is why you eat today with us. In Pashtunwali, we call this *melmastia*—hospitality."

"And when we leave, I ask that you provide us with *nanawatai*." Declan placed his cup of chai on the ground near his side. "Protection. You see, we came here in peace. We ask that we leave in peace. We do not want to harm anyone."

The tribal leader seemed impressed by both his understanding of Islam and his understanding of the Pashtun honor code.

"Collins, we need to head out." Hooch headed toward Declan's mini-jirga. "Choppers are en route."

Declan and Griff prepared for exfil. The elders followed their lead, standing tall. Declan said no more, not even a goodbye. He knew that although the elders had treated them to some chai, that didn't mean friendships had been won.

"They claim the four captured are not Taliban," Awarang said, attempting to translate some mild commotion coming from the elders.

"So that's why they treated us." Declan finished kitting himself back up. "Someone in the group cares about one of our tangos. Keep walking."

Just then, he felt a sudden tug on his shirtsleeve. With an adrenaline surge from the unexpected pull, he turned his head and stared right into the green eyes of the village chief.

"He claims the guy wearing the boots is his son." Awarang pointed to one of the four captured suspects.

"Keep walking." At the sight of the boots, Declan became unglued. "They're French-military issued."

"What do you want to do?" Griff asked.

"Nothing." He continued walking back to the remaining force. "Nothing we can do. We know the guy is a terrorist. The elder knows it too. Nothing more can be done unless we're willing to round up the entire village, knowing every one of them is Taliban."

"That isn't happening," Rex said, out of breath. He had finally caught back up with them. "Would you believe this fiasco?"

"What?" Declan asked while keeping an eye on the villagers he had just left.

"This is supposed to be SF." Rex pointed at a handful of men resting on the ground. "This LZ isn't secured. No one is pulling security. You have a wheat field on one side, a village on the other, and mountains all around us."

"Let me grab some guys." Griff sped off, seeking some bodies to help pull security.

The sound of incoming helicopters was getting clearer. Declan could tell Rex was uneasy that the incoming birds didn't have the location secured adequately.

"Follow me," Rex shouted while moving toward a footpath leading up the mountain behind the village.

Six men followed. All of them were advisors and JSOC elements, except for Griff, who was SF. A quarter of the way up the mountain, yet only a stone's throw away from the landing zone, they took a hasty security posture. Declan remained high on adrenaline.

One Chinook landed. Four captured Taliban boarded with a handful of ANA commandos and US Special Forces. Multiple birds hovered overhead providing aerial security. A cloud of wheat filled the air due to the prop wash. Declan noticed something move a hundred yards in front of him.

"I think we might have some contact," he shouted as he raised the sites of his weapon.

"Tattoo, you have three tangos moving your direction," Rex called to his Philippine counterpart.

Heavy weapon fire unleashed from the heavens above into the mountainside. The first Chinook took off while another landed. Air cover was used to keep the enemy's head down until everyone was lifted out of the landing zone. Declan knew he and his teammates would be the last ones out.

"We need to move," Rex shouted to his men.

"You guys go," Griff called back. "We'll bound behind you." He unleashed several rounds of three-round burst in the direction of the enemy.

"Moving," Rex bellowed as he, Declan, and Captain Jack retreated closer to the landing zone.

Shots fired. The difference in sound between AK and M-4 rounds was obvious. Griff was in a skirmish.

"Griff, get the hell out of there," Declan called over the radio while taking cover close to the landing zone's edge.

Tattoo ran toward him. Brett followed his lead. Shrek was next.

"Where's Griff?" Declan demanded.

"C'mon," Captain Jack ordered, and began running back towards Griff's last-known location.

"Big Red 1, we need some help down here." Rex announced to Apache air support overhead.

"Roger that, Raven 1. Doing some passes now. You have five bodies on the ground. Looks like all KIA. We don't see any hostiles."

"Griff's been shot," Tattoo relayed over the net. "I need a medic down here ASAP."

Declan and Rex rushed to catch up to Captain Jack and his small contingent. Shrek was huddled near Griff's body, trying to stabilize him, as he choked out blood. Quick security postures were taken by all the men, except Shrek, who continued trying to resuscitate the downed Special Forces member.

"I have no pulse," Shrek barked as he began punching Griff's chest.

"Griff." Declan choked. His friend was on the ground, his body lifeless.

"Let's go," Captain Jack ordered. "Shrek, Tattoo, get him on that damn chopper."

"We gotta save him, Captain," Declan cried out.

At his side, Rex said, "He's gone."

TWENTY-SEVEN

A plume of dust filled the air. Medical vehicles awaited the return of a contingent of US special operators. The team was exhausted. Declan, like the others, was grieving the loss of a teammate. At least only a couple of months remained before he would be home again in Brannagh's arms.

"Where are you going?" Rex asked Declan as the men headed in the direction of the tactical operations center. "No, no. You need to see the docs."

"I can't even be part of the debrief?" Declan asked while painfully turning his head to look at Rex. "The med tent is part of the morgue. I can't be in there right now knowing Griff is there."

"Understood." Rex placed his arm around him. "We'll have Colonel Crooner check you out. He's Brigade's head doc and likely hanging out in the TOC."

The tactical operations center was filled with analysts and decision makers. As Hooch, Captain Jack, Rex, and Declan walked in, Declan knew they looked like characters from the *Night of the Living Dead*. Colonel Davis, the Brigade deputy commander, greeted them with unexpected positivity. Declan was taken aback, unsure whether Colonel Davis realized what they had just gone through.

"Give me some lovin'." Colonel Davis placed his hand in the air for a series of high fives. "You men really took it to them. I'm proud of you."

"Four HVTs captured and a handful of enemy KIA," Hooch replied, gesturing toward a live stream of unmanned aerial vehicle footage of the AF/PAK border crossing of Torkham Gate. "We lost one of our own, sir."

"What?" Colonel Davis appeared confused. His eyes squinted as he tapped his fingers on his forehead. "How come we didn't hear anything over the net? When did this happen? How?"

Declan felt a sudden surge of nausea. "I need some water," he said.

"During exfiltration." Captain Jack replied while running his fingers across his bearded chin.

The colonel, quick on his feet, knew to get the men out of clear view of the busy bees working inside the TOC. He hurried them into his office and shut the door behind as they entered.

"Staff Sergeant Raymond Griffin," Hooch blurted as the team walked into Colonel Davis's office. "He was our S2. Our only ASOT Level III-certified guy. Best intelligence officer I ever had under my command."

All five of them took a seat, heads hung low. Declan's nausea passed after he downed a bottle of water, but his mind still moved a million miles an hour.

He lifted his left arm over his head, trying to relieve the poignant pain running through his elbow. "As crazy as this sounds, I think we need to go back."

"For what?" Captain Jack asked.

"Intel. We can plant a cache of weapons nearby. Do it so the villagers will find them. Plant the cache with some tracking devices."

"Actually, that makes perfect sense." Rex jumped to his support.

"Sir," Declan blurted, looking directly at Colonel Davis. "We were just in Indian country. The entire village is Taliban controlled. The place is more than likely a rest, recoup, and recover location for Taliban."

"With the right tools, we can track who's going in and out." Rex added, excited, as he always was, when Declan thought outside of the box. "If we do what he's saying, we have a much higher chance of tracking the enemy. No boots would be needed on the ground."

"An air drop?" Colonel Davis asked, interested now.

"Possibly," Declan said. "I don't know how we should go about doing it, but I do know we should."

"Air drop won't work," Captain Jack explained. "You would still need a team to go in and set it all up the right way. Personally, I don't believe the colonel has access to those types of tools."

"But you do." Hooch whirled to Captain Jack. "If you guys can't do it, will you allow my guys?"

"You know those tools are only designated for tier one and two high-value targets." Captain Jack crossed his arms. "I'm sure my guys wouldn't say anything, though, if some of those tracking devices miraculously went missing. Let me see if I can throw some underground sensors in the package. That's what you really need for this."

Declan tried to stretch his neck without being noticed.

"You hurting?" Colonel Davis asked. So much for that.

"I'm okay."

"Speaking of," Rex interjected. "Is Doc Crooner in his office?"

"Yeah," Colonel Davis said.

"Go, Declan." Rex pointed across the room toward the doc's office. "Go see Colonel Crooner." Declan shook Colonel Davis's hand and headed out the door. He would have given anything to stay. He sure as hell wanted to stay in the loop of any payback planned for the village. But something was wrong, really wrong, with his neck.

✝✝✝

Declan walked through the door of Colonel Crooner's office. "Hey, Doc. Got a second?"

"Hey there, Declan." Doc Crooner grinned. "Tell your wife how happy I was to get some of those cigars she shipped over to you."

"Next time I speak to her I'll ask her to send some more." Declan felt himself smile for the first time in several hours.

"So what's going on?" Doc placed the most recent issue of *Sports Illustrated* on his desk. He kept the magazine in his office regularly to pass some time when he wasn't seeing patients.

"I was on that helo that went down." Declan tried to sound matter-of-fact. "Ever since, I can't get rid of these pins and needles in my left arm."

"Your neck is messed up," the doc said. "You need an MRI. Unfortunately, we don't have that type of equipment here."

"Bagram?" Declan asked.

"Nope. They don't have one either. No one in country does. We have to fly you out to Germany."

"That's not happening, Doc. I'd be out of pocket for at least two weeks. Can't do that."

"How do your legs feel?" He began tapping Declan's knees with a tiny hammer.

"No problems. My reflexes are fine."

"How much longer do you have in country?"

"About two months, give or take."

"Listen, son." Doc Crooner started looking concerned. "You have a wife back home. You're no longer in the military. If you don't take care of yourself, you may never go home walking."

"That bad?" Declan swallowed the lump in his throat.

"That bad," he said. "I think you either herniated a disk, or worse, you may have actually broken your neck."

"C'mon, Doc."

"I'm serious." He opened up a cabinet behind him. "You're going to be really sore in the morning. Here's eight hundred milligrams of Motrin. I would give you some Percocet, but I don't want you going outside the wire too doped up."

"Well, if it really gets as bad as you say, I know where to find you." He took the container of Motrin. "Thanks for your time."

"Just a minute." The doc stopped Declan from walking out of his office. "I can't tell you what to do, but if you were in the military, and I was your doctor, I would have you on a MEDVAC and sent to the hospital in Stuttgart."

"Give me a number," Declan told him. "How many cigars will this cost me?"

"None." Doc Crooner frowned. "You stay in Afghanistan until your time's up if you want. I only ask that you don't go outside the wire until you get cleared to do so, after an MRI."

"Two months sitting behind a desk," he said as he walked out the door. Two months thinking about Griff's senseless death, and the fact that he couldn't do anything about it. "This sucks."

"You're only one man. This war will continue with or without you. Don't be a hero. I've seen too many heroes in this world, and they're all six feet deep."

His comment struck Declan like a dagger into his heart. "Two months sitting behind a desk," Declan said again as he walked out the door. "Can you keep this just between you and me? I can't go home just yet, but I promise in two months I'll do exactly as you say."

Doc Crooner was silent but nodded.

Hooch, Captain Jack, and Rex were walking out of Colonel Davis's office. They appeared to be in decent spirits considering the circumstances.

"Going to chow. Want to come with us?" Rex asked as he gestured toward the exit of the TOC.

"Sure."

"So what did the doc say?" Captain Jack asked as he opened the door for the men.

"I'm a FOBBIT for the next two months." Declan walked out into the evening sunset of eastern Afghanistan.

"What?" Rex asked in shock.

"Yup. He wants me to get an MRI, but I can't here in Afghanistan." He put on his sunglasses. "He thinks I either herniated a disk or broke my neck."

"No way!" Rex blurted.

"Yeah," Hooch chimed in. "I know guys who got broken necks on jumps, and you would never tell by looking at them."

They entered the chow tent, and Declan picked up a dinner plate. "Don't worry, Rex. I told him I couldn't leave you as a one-man wrecking crew. Told him I would stay until my tour's over."

"And he was good with that?" Rex asked as he gestured to the server for some corn with his grilled chicken breast.

"Personally, I think he thinks guys like us are crazy." Declan grabbed some fresh rolls. "I think he likes having guys like us around."

"Yeah, we're real entertainment for some of these folks," Rex said and moved down the food line.

"Either way, I'm now FOB ridden," Declan said and looked for an empty table. "A bloody FOBBIT."

Secretly, Declan was livid. He didn't want to see his guys go outside the wire without him. This is what he believed he was meant to do in his life, but all likelihood of carrying out his beliefs had come crumbling down like an avalanche.

TWENTY-EIGHT

A burning sensation ran through Declan's left arm. Waking at dawn to meet Rex at Brigade's daily morning brief was excruciating. His neck was stiff, his body was sore, and he was mentally exhausted.

Griff's death was all he could think about. He needed to talk to Rex and level with him about what was going on in his head. Rex had spent plenty of time in conflict zones. Losing a friend in times of war wasn't easy, but if anyone knew how to deal with the demons, Rex was that person.

Colonel Davis entered the tactical operations center, clean-shaven and meticulous as always. When he spotted Declan, his usually jovial expression grew serious.

"Where's your partner in crime?" The full bird gave him a hug and a look that conveyed his unspoken sympathy.

"I thought he was already here." Declan scanned the room and searched for Rex.

"This isn't like him," Colonel Davis said. "Give him five minutes. If he doesn't show up, go looking for him."

Five minutes passed. The daily brief began, and Rex was still nowhere in sight. Colonel Davis nodded to Declan and gestured toward the door.

First Declan checked the team room. It was vacant. Rex wasn't in the chow hall, he wasn't in the latrines, and he wasn't in his hooch. There was only one place Declan hadn't looked. The gym. He should have thought of that first. It was what Rex did when other guys hit the bottle. He was trying to deal with what had happened in his own way.

Rex didn't believe in traditional workouts. He had tucked a little makeshift gym of his own discretely behind his sleeping quarters. As Declan walked between the tents, he could hear deep huffing and puffing. The noises sounded like they were coming from a crazed beast finalizing a kill.

"Hey, Brother, you missed the morning brief." Declan lifted an old heavy bag off the ground.

Rex didn't answer. Shirtless and sweaty, he was busy throwing sandbags. Declan waited for him to finish his exercise before continuing.

A plume of dust filled the air as Rex threw the final sandbag in front of his feet. "Screw those daily briefs," he said.

"Rex, what's going on?"

"What's going on?" He grabbed a bottle of water and gulped. "This entire mission, it's completely FUBARed. That's what's going on."

Declan had never seen his team leader so disgusted. Everyone was hurting, but Rex showed something more than mental anguish. He was starting to show signs of quitting, and Declan couldn't let that happen.

"Talk to me, Brother."

"Sorry, man." He pulled himself up on the chin bar. "We're a team, and I wasn't there for you this morning after we all just went through hell."

"Nothing to be sorry about. I know you need time. And working out is your stress reliever."

"Whatever." Rex continued his set of pull-ups.

"If that's the way you want it." Declan picked up an old tent poll and began striking Rex in the gut every time he lowered himself into the pull-up rest position. "You need to snap out of it, or I'm going to hit you harder with this thing."

Rex barked as Declan cracked him one more time. "It's an added stomach workout, that's all. When I get back to the States, and your beautiful wife hooks me up with one of her friends, she'll drool over my abs."

Declan began to laugh, and finally, unable to do another pull-up, Rex joined him. The tension was broken.

"You know, I left Special Forces once I saw how lazy they were getting," Rex said as he put on his T-shirt. "They're supposed to be the best. In the past forty-eight hours, they just proved all my old suspicions. They no longer take care of the little things. They just want to be hero door-kicker types. It's all about direct action for them."

"What's your point?" Declan asked. "And how does any of this have to do with the past forty-eight hours?"

"Who were the first ones on those helos?" he demanded.

"SF." Special Forces, the Green Berets.

"Exactly." Rex wiped some sweat out of his eyes. "They should have been the first ones going up that ridgeline, providing cover for exfil. Not Captain Jack's guys, not us, and sure as hell not Griff. He was their S2, for Christ sake."

"Would of, could of, should of," Declan said. "We can Monday-morning-quarterback yesterday's situation all we want. That's not going to bring Griff back."

"Yeah, but how many more times will this happen in the future?" Rex grabbed his backpack, ready to head toward the office.

171

"So everything is FUBAR. What do you want to do? Go home?"

"Home?" Rex's chuckle was bitter. "And where is that? When I'm in the States, I live out of a Winnebago. Unlike you, I don't have a home. This is it."

"Oh, I see. So, Afghanistan's your new home?"

"Not necessarily Afghanistan. Anywhere the wars are fought. This is how I make my living."

"And what happens when the wars are over?" Declan asked.

"There's always a war somewhere."

Declan knew he was right. At no time in history did the world ever have a complete day of peace. Somewhere in a far-off land, someone was being killed by some rogue regime.

Africa, Asia, South America, Rex could pick and choose where he wanted to make money as a mercenary. Declan knew that, in Rex's eyes, that's exactly what he was. Nothing derogatory about it. Rex wanted that task. He wanted to do his job and get paid for his work. He didn't see it any differently than a corporate position. In fact, he saw himself as more ethical than the big corporate snakes stealing money from consumers.

Declan didn't care about the war effort or the money to be made. He cared about serving alongside that brotherhood only found in a war zone. Sure, the money was the icing on the cake, but more than that, he needed to be here.

As they walked back to join the others, his left arm felt as if it had caught fire. It burned from the inside out.

Rex spotted his discomfort at once. "What's wrong?" he asked.

"Nothing that can't be fixed," Declan told him.

It was more than a self-diagnosis, more than a way to appease Rex's curiosity. To Declan, it was a fervent hope. The pain was worse than anything he had experienced, and in order to do his job, he was going to have to deal with it. And soon.

TWENTY-NINE

Tears fell on Brannagh's cheeks. After placing the phone back on the nightstand, she turned her body deep into that of her faithful companion, Apoc, and hugged her dog for much needed love. The telephone conversation had left her terrified.

Dear God, don't let him do anything stupid, she thought as she watched the morning sunrise through her bedroom window. Grabbing a nearby tissue to wipe her tears, Brannagh reflected on last night's evening news. *One US helicopter downed by insurgents, leaving one dead.* He hadn't told her everything. Maybe the news didn't have the correct information. What was really going on over there?

Caitlin, though back in New Jersey, was only a phone call away. Brannagh needed an ear. Her sister was her closest confidant.

"Cat, its Bran."

"Oh my God, what time is it?" Caitlin muttered. "What's going on?"

"Did you see the news last night?" Brannagh asked while she turned on the television.

"No." Caitlin replied. "We were out baby shopping. I'm getting out of bed right now."

"Turn on the news."

"OK, it's on."

"You see the helo they keep putting up on the screen?" she said, as tears flooded her eyes. "Declan was on it."

"Bran, you heard from him, though, right?" Caitlin asked. "Tell me you heard from him and that he's all right."

"We just got off the phone before I called you. He claims he's OK, just a bit sore."

"Sweetie, if he said he's OK, I am sure he is. I'm going downstairs to grab an early morning cup of coffee."

"No, he didn't tell me everything." Brannagh glanced from the news to the wedding photo on the dresser. "Something isn't right. I can just feel it."

"Bran, the news is saying an American GI was killed over there," Caitlin said. "Was the GI killed in the crash?"

"I don't know," she replied. "The report doesn't make any sense. How could someone have been killed in a crash, but Declan comes out unscathed?"

"Wait a second," Caitlin said. "Now, they're saying it was a firefight. The GI was killed in a firefight. It had to be a separate incident."

"No, Declan told me they lost one of their own." Brannagh flipped the channels, trying to see what Caitlin saw. "Declan was there. It all took place at the same time."

"Are they flying him out of country for medical treatment?" Caitlin asked. "I heard that when guys get injured over there, the military often flies them out to Germany."

"No, he said he's sore. That's it."

"Bran, you have to trust him on this one or you'll drive yourself nuts. You have no reason not to trust him, right?"

"It's what we talked about when you and Joe were here," she admitted. "I don't even know who he works for. It's like his life is one big secret."

"Honey, no. It's like you said. He works for the government."

"But which government?"

"What does that mean?"

"The federal government or the private one? I don't know if he's working directly for the Fed or as a contractor. I didn't feel right asking…"

"Contractors work for the government," Caitlin said too quickly.

"Yeah, I know. But when contractors get injured, they get the royal shaft."

"How so if he has insurance?" Caitlin asked.

"Plausible deniability," she said.

Bran was innocent but her innocence was not to be confused with ignorance. Being married to Declan had enlightened her enough that she understood some of the consequences that come with working in war zones. She could only pray those consequences wouldn't affect her husband's well-being.

Because of the possibility that Declan was a contractor, Bran feared the atrocities that frequently unfolded among injured contractors and their employers. She knew many contractors never received medical benefits even though they paid the mandated insurance needed to operate abroad. She also knew the government didn't take responsibility for contractual casualties because the contractors were employed by private businesses even though most of the money came straight out of government funds.

Bran knew about this thing called the Defense Base Act (DBA). She knew how corrupt it truly was. This was only one more danger facing contractors. Getting injured or killed overseas was one danger. Facing the dreaded Defense Base Act was another. She wondered whether Declan would be forced to face a calamity of legal issues revolving around the DBA. Only time would tell.

PART IV

THIRTY

Agitated that Doc Crooner had sold him out, Declan finally boarded the aircraft that would eventually bring him back to Brannagh. He couldn't believe that the doc would actually go behind his back about his injury. He kept picturing the doc's face when both men agreed that, in two months, Declan would return home and get checked out. Declan felt betrayed. At least he would be stateside in time to pay his respects to Griff.

Just before boarding his plane, Declan sent a quick message to Bran, telling her that he was on his way. He asked her to get down to DC with some suits and casual wear. They were going to a funeral.

There was no time to go home first. He believed being with Griff one last time was more important, and surely Bran would understand. A day of flying back to the States, a night in a hotel, and the next morning at Arlington National Cemetery would be exhausting, but for Declan, it was just another day in the office.

By eight-thirty in the morning, he had been awake for six hours. Staff Sergeant Raymond Griffin's body would be the first laid to rest, at precisely nine o'clock. Morning dew blanketed the ground. As he stepped into the cemetery a wave of nausea hit Declan. Letting go of Bran's hand, he stopped mid pace and took a deep breath.

"Are you OK?" she asked.

"I will be." He reached for her hand, and they walked closer to the burial site.

A crowd surrounded Griff's casket. Uniformed Green Berets gathered with their spouses in one group. Next to them, stood a handful of burly men wearing suits and black sunglasses. They were likely members of the prestigious First Special Forces Operational Detachment Delta commonly referred to as Delta Force. Griff's grandparents, mother, and father sat with Merry, his young widow, and Sean, his three-year-old son. Bran couldn't stop looking at Griff's little boy.

Birds flew aimlessly in the blue sky. Declan braced himself for what he knew was coming next. Three volleys honoring Griff were fired into the air, and the birds scattered. Bran jumped, along with Griff's family members.

The honor guard meticulously folded the flag in its triangular shape, placing three shell casings inside. The flag was handed over to Griff's sobbing wife. His boy never shed a tear. Bran's tears flowed for him.

"It's over." He hugged her. "C'mon."

She had no words. Silence buffered the two as they walked from the burial site. Wiping away tears, Bran looked at him with unspoken questions in her eyes.

"I noticed you from across the casket." A hand gripped Declan's left elbow. "You don't remember me."

Declan turned only to see a face without a name. "I'm sorry, sir. You look very familiar."

"Philadelphia International Airport. Drinking my breakfast."

"Yes." Declan released his hand from Bran's. "I don't believe we ever got one another's name that day."

He and the suit shook hands. "Please, call me Charles."

Declan felt the slip of a business card inside his right hand. Knowing not to look down at it, he replied, "Declan. Declan Collins."

"Well, it's unfortunate we had to reconnect this way, but it's nice seeing you again." Charles turned and walked off. Meeting adjourned. They were professionals, and they both knew that Griff's funeral wasn't the time or place to speak more.

"Who was that?" Bran asked as they arrived at the car.

He opened her door and replied, "I'm not sure yet." With keys in hand, he paused for a moment after sitting in the driver's seat. "I have to go back."

"Go back?" she asked in complete shock. "What do you mean you have to go back?"

"This isn't over." He placed the keys in the ignition. "I need to get medically cleared then get back over there."

"I don't believe this." Bran hid her face in her hands, and he knew she was crying. "What about us?"

"There would be no us if it weren't for guys like Griff and those who're still in country fighting," he told her. "America is in a war. It's the longest war in our country's history. My brothers are over there fighting. They need me."

Brannagh's hands slapped down into her lap. "No. Declan, I need you. Don't you want that family we always dreamed of? Did you see Griff's son? Who's going to teach him how to shave? Who's going to teach him how to throw a football? Who's going to fill Griff's role as his daddy? Who would fill your role if something happened to you?"

"Can we talk about this later?" he asked. "We need to go be with the guys. I promise, we won't be long, just enough time to show our support, have a drink, and we can leave."

"A drink?" Bran looked into the passenger's visor mirror and touched up her runny mascara. "It's not even noon."

"It's five o'clock somewhere," he said.

Though it was mid-morning on the East Coast, for Declan it was really late night. For the Special Forces members in attendance, time meant nothing. They were twenty-four-hour-a-day operators who did whatever needed to be done, no matter the hour. Declan knew this and felt, no matter what time it was, that a quick toast to his departed brother was essential.

THIRTY-ONE

D eclan knew Griff would have been proud that so many warriors were celebrating his life. A shrine with his photo, dog tags, boots, and weapon had been placed on a table next to the bar. Each man who received a drink tapped his glass, in the form of a toast, on the picture's frame.

Declan was acquainted with only a handful of the men present at the wake. Beside him, Bran appeared calm and respectful. Yet she stared at the curly-red-haired boy who pranced around unaware that his father would never return.

"Dec, what do you say?" she asked. "Should we get going?"

"Yeah, sweetie, I think we've been here long enough." He grabbed her hand. "Let's just say goodbye."

They walked over to Merry, Griff's widow, and shared their condolences one last time. Little Sean was near.

"Come here, you little cutie." Bran bent down and opened up her arms. "Can I get a hug?"

Sean, with his white button-down shirt half tucked inside his suit pants, looked at his mother as if to ask who this stranger was. Merry gestured for him to hug Bran. Without a word, he threw himself into Bran's arms.

"Come on, hon, we have to leave." Declan placed his hand under Bran's arm and helped her up.

The two walked out the door, and he knew she was holding in tears. "Declan, promise me you'll never put me through that," she whispered.

"Not now, Bran. Let's not discuss this right now."

"When?"

Declan was in no mood. He couldn't stop thinking about that last operation he and Griff were on. He couldn't stop thinking about the little things, like the first time the two ever spoke, or the time when Griff almost swallowed his chewing tobacco because he was laughing so hard at Rex's comments to Major Franks. Most of all, he kept thinking about the heroism Griff displayed that day he died, as he stormed up that Afghan hillside, fighting off the enemy so his brothers would return safely to base.

"When our heads are clearer," he said. "We both just went through a mental roller coaster. Let's get out of here."

"OK." Bran wiped the last tear from her face. "Can we just go back to the hotel?"

"Of course."

The O'Callaghan Hotel in Annapolis, Maryland, was where they had stayed on their first little getaway as a couple. Although it wasn't the greatest hotel in Annapolis, with its rustic feel, it reminded them of Ireland. They walked into the room, and Bran said, "I'm going to soak in the tub for a little while. Do you mind?"

"Of course not. I know you need to relax. I'm just going to sit here and try to numb my mind. Our emotions have been running wild today."

"Emotions, yeah. Hormones, possibly." She paused, and then went into the bathroom. Declan turned on the television.

He missed watching major news networks. In Afghanistan, he was limited to the Armed Forces Network or CNN International.

As Bran ran a bath, he knew he had some time. He pulled out his smart-phone to reach out to a long-lost friend.

"So should I keep calling you Spartacus now that I'm back, or can I call you Earl?" he joked.

"So you're back?" Earl Flanders replied. "You back in Pennsy?"

"Actually, we're right around the corner from you." Declan tweaked open the blind and peeked outside the window.

Although he knew better, he couldn't help checking whether any surveillance was being conducted on him from street level. There was no reason for him to feel threatened. He was home safe and sound, but his security-conscious mind would always churn.

"You're in Annapolis?"

"Yeah, I tried calling you before I left the Stan, but I couldn't get through. My layover in Dubai was too short, so I figured I would call you when I landed. But things got hectic."

"What the hell are you doing down here?"

"Funeral." Declan stretched out on the bed. "Remember the S2 from Third Group I told you about? My arrival here in the States got me back in time to say my last goodbye."

"Is Bran down here with you?"

"Yeah. She isn't doing too well." Declan pulled the phone from his ear to be sure the water was still running. "She's never been to one before. A full-service military funeral. It was tough on her. She can't stop thinking about Griff's little boy."

"It's not easy, especially the first time," Earl said. "You guys going to stay the night?"

"Yeah, she's taking a bath now." Declan heard the water shut off.

"Let me tell Vicki you're in town. We'll meet you down at the lobby around five." Earl talked faster, unable to hide the eagerness in his voice. "You're staying at the O'Callaghan, right?"

"Yeah." Declan walked farther away from the bathroom, trying to keep Bran from overhearing the conversation. "Earl, she's never met you two. I don't know how she'll feel about going out to dinner tonight with two strangers."

"Nonsense. We're not strangers," Earl blurted. "It's time she and I met."

"I don't know. She was really shaken earlier. Can I at least discuss this with her?" The phone went silent.

"Earl? Earl, are you still there?"

Of course not. His mentor was off planning their evening. They shared a forever bond, and Earl considered Bran part of the family.

As he waited for Bran, he must have fallen asleep. Something warm and fragrant awakened him. Bran, with tiny beads of water stuck to her damp naked body, covered his neck with soft kisses.

"What are you doing?" he moaned, still half-asleep.

"Shhh," Bran whispered in his ear and moved on top of him.

He gently caressed her breasts, and she leaned back with her hands pressed against his chest.

Together, they tried to love away the pain. With her, the funeral was only a sad memory now. There was no death. Only life. In her arms, he could believe again. He could think about the future. Soon they'd be together like this every night. They could start that family they both wanted.

"I love you, Declan Collins." She leaned down and kissed his lips.

"I love you, Bran."

She placed her head on his chest and ran her fingers up and down his body. He buried his face in her hair, smelling the soft fragrance of wildflowers.

"You should take a bath more often when I'm around."

"I might just have to take another one." She rose up, and her dark hair brushed his face. "Or do you want to just stay here and order something from room service?"

"No can do." He continued caressing her hair. "I talked to Earl when you were in the tub. He and Vicki want to link up with us for dinner."

"You've got to be kidding me, right?" She grew rigid in his arms. "Tonight?"

"We don't make it down here together very often," he said. "He still feels terrible that Vicki and he couldn't make it to our wedding. He's family, Bran."

"So am I." She met his eyes. "Baby, I wanted you all to myself tonight."

"You'll have an entire lifetime with me, sweetie."

"I sure hope so." Her eyes filled with tears. "Griff didn't have an entire lifetime with anyone. Not Merry, not…"

"Please don't." He didn't want to hear another word. He couldn't. "Griff believed in what he was doing. I believe in what I'm doing. And when this is over, it's going to be you and me and as many kids as you want. You know I wouldn't lie to you about something that important."

"No, but…"

He pulled her closer, loving her warmth and the touch of her baby-soft skin. "But what, Irish woman?"

That got a smile. "Nothing." She sighed. "Now, I guess it's time for me to get dressed and meet that mentor of yours, the great Spartacus."

"You'll be the most beautiful woman in the restaurant."

"And you'll be the hottest guy, Dec."

She gave him a kiss that was almost as warm and trusting as the one with which she'd awakened him. With Bran in his arms, he felt alive again. He felt like a man, a man with an amazingly beautiful woman by his side. In spite of all that had happened, he couldn't be happier.

THIRTY-TWO

Declan and Bran accidentally fell asleep in each other's arms. Declan's mind went blank. No dreams of Afghanistan, none of Griff's funeral, no dreams remembered at all. He was in a state of complete peace, happy.

They awakened for a second round of heated lovemaking.

"I could do this all night." Bran rolled over, gasping for air. "Oh my God, Dec, look at the time. It's ten till five."

"Shit." Declan jumped off the bed, naked. "I need to take a shower."

The shower water massaged Declan's body. Bran couldn't resist. She slipped into the steamy room where he was covered with a thick soapy lather.

"Here, let me wash you." With one hand, she stroked a washcloth across his back. With her free hand, she ran her fingers down his chest and began kissing the back of his neck. As aroused as he was, time was not on their side.

"Baby, we really need to hurry," he whispered. "Let's continue this after dinner."

"I'll try to wait. No guarantees, though."

"I'll run down to the lobby." Declan reached for a towel. "You do your thing. Just don't be too long."

"Can you buy me fifteen minutes?" Bran asked as she tapped his butt.

Declan threw on a pair of light-gray slacks and a white button-down. His hair wasn't fully dry as he stormed out of the room. With smartphone in hand, he saw the text from Earl. *We're here.* It had been sent five minutes before.

He took the stairs down to the lobby instead of waiting for the outdated elevator. The lobby was around the corner. Poised, Declan stopped and took a deep breath in an attempt to hide any sense of urgency. He spotted his silver-haired friend wearing a formal navy blue blazer with bronze buttons and a white dress shirt as if he were the captain of a luxurious sailboat. Vicki was by Earl's side, dressed in an elegant summer floral dress. The two were speaking with the hotel's bartender.

Vicki was first to see him. She threw open her arms and called out, "Declan."

He hugged her soundly. "Hey, Vicki, you look great."

Earl turned from the bar and looked at Declan with a sigh of relief. "Hey, Brother."

They embraced one another for several seconds before Earl glanced back at the bartender.

"Hey, Fast Eddie, anything this guy wants, hook him up. He's a combat hero, Eddie. Just got back from Afghanistan."

While this was indeed a celebration, Declan knew that even when Earl celebrated, he conducted business. The normal celebratory drink, rum and coke, would let their hair down too much, so Declan ordered his favorite scotch. "Macallan's, please, on the rocks."

"You look good." Earl couldn't wipe the smile from his face. "Where's your better half?"

Declan turned. The elevator doors opened. Bran walked out wearing a white sundress with a hint of lace showing at the knee. Her brown hair flowed over one shoulder, setting off her great bone structure. With drink in hand, Declan tapped Earl on the arm.

Vicki and Earl both turned.

"Oh my God, Declan, she could be in a magazine," Vicki said.

"That's for sure," Earl agreed. "I wouldn't have made it out of the room if I had her in bed with me."

Vicki punched Earl on the shoulder. "Stop drooling. You're stuck with me."

"Stuck? Baby, I'm honored to be with a woman like you." Earl leaned over and kissed her on the cheek.

Declan remained in awe. He reached for his angel's hand and gently leaned into her ear. "You look amazing."

"Vicki, Earl, this is Brannagh."

"Please, call me Bran."

Vicki and Bran bonded immediately. That didn't surprise Declan. Vicki had spent the past twenty-plus years living a life similar to the one Bran had just been introduced to. Husband always abroad in some unknown third-world country, never knowing where he was, never knowing if he would come home alive, and never knowing exactly what he was doing.

It was a great start to a wonderful and much needed relaxing evening. "Vicki and I want to take you two lovebirds out to our favorite restaurant." Earl reached around Vicki's waist and pulled her next to him. "You two like Italian?"

"Italian? Annapolis doesn't have real Italian food," Declan joked, knowing Earl was thinking of Carpino's Italian restaurant. To Bran, he added, "We've debated for years whether Annapolis or Philly has better Italian food."

"I thought Annapolis was a crab cake town?" Bran said with sincere innocence.

"Sweetie, you're going to love this place." Vicki gently grabbed her hand. "We women will walk together."

Bran turned, looking back at Declan as Vicki pulled her out the door. Her smile was as bright as day, giddy she was in the company of such amazing people. Declan winked at her, as if to say, *I told you you'd love these folks.*

"Don't walk too far ahead," Earl demanded. "I would hate to have to kill some dirtballs for disrespecting two incredibly gorgeous women with their eyes."

"Let them go," Declan said quietly. "It might be the only time we have to discuss some things tonight."

"Something on your mind?"

"Well, a lot of things are on my mind, but one more than the others. I ran into this guy, twice now. Once at the airport a couple of months ago, and then again at Griff's funeral." Declan reached into his pocket and pulled out a business card. "Ever hear of a guy by the name of Charles Becker?"

"Charles Becker?" Earl waited at the lobby door they were exiting, allowing a couple of young Annapolis Midshipmen to walk by. "Yeah, I know him. I know him well. His name doesn't ring a bell to you?"

"Not one bit."

"You're a typical operator, Dec. That's a good thing." Earl said as their wives neared Carpino's front doors. "He's a good friend. Former Under SECDEF for intel. He and I see one another about two or three times a year at events."

"Interesting that he and I just so happened to run into one another on two separate occasions." Declan stopped at the restaurant door. "Wonder if those encounters were intentional."

"Probably not intentional." Earl faced him. "But I assure you that the next time you two do see one another, I'll be around."

"Well, he gave me his card." Declan handed it to Earl. "I take it that he wants me to contact him."

"Send him an e-mail." Earl handed the card back. "Keep it short and simple. Just thank him for going to the funeral. Don't ask any questions, and don't give him anything either. Just a line or two. Let him respond. Then we'll take it from there."

With that, the two of them walked inside the restaurant. How different it was from the world Declan had just left. From the white tablecloths to the dim lights to the dark walnut bar, it was just what he needed. Very few patrons sat inside, as it was still relatively early for a big Annapolis crowd.

"Red or white wine?" Vicki asked Bran.

"Either is fine. I think I'll start with club soda."

"Sure thing. What about you, Dec?"

"Red's fine. Bran will probably want some later on."

"Sweet or dry?"

"Dry?" he asked and looked at Bran. She nodded.

A waiter arrived to take drink orders as Declan and Earl sat next to their wives. With the waiter came Carpino's owner, Raf. "Earl, Vicki, it's nice seeing you as always. Declan, it's been a long time. And may I ask who this lovely lady is?"

"Raf, it's been about a year." Declan stood, shaking his hand. "This is my wife, Bran."

"Madam, it is a true pleasure to meet you." Raf reached out for her hand and kissed it as if he were some European maître d'. "Declan, you're quite the lucky man."

"Trust me, I know." He kissed Bran on the cheek.

"What brings you to Annapolis?" He pointed to Earl. "Tell me you didn't come here just to see this guy?"

"Dec just returned from Afghanistan," Earl told him. "Flew into BWI a couple of days ago."

"Welcome home," Raf said. "So this is a special occasion. Let me make sure we celebrate it properly."

He walked back to the kitchen as if on a mission. The Malbec Cabernet Franc arrived, and Earl lifted his glass.

"Welcome home, my friend."

"Yes, welcome home, Declan." Vicki looked over to Bran. "And to finally getting to meet your gorgeous wife."

Raf returned. "No menus tonight," he said. "I have some fresh veal, seafood, pasta, salad, soup, and dessert being prepared. I assure you that you will love everything."

Declan could see that Bran's earlier worries had vanished. He tried his best to hide that he thought of his brothers whom he'd left behind in Afghanistan. Memories of those men constantly filled his head, as did the whole war. He was home, though, and allowing such thoughts to interfere with time spent among friends wasn't healthy.

"I'm going to run to the ladies room before the food gets here." Vicki slid away from the table.

"I'll join you," Bran replied.

With their wives gone, Earl got to the point. He no longer bothered trying to hide his concern. "How are you holding up?"

"You know what happened, right?" Declan asked. "Why I'm back here and not still in the Stan?"

"Your neck?"

"Yeah, Doc sold me out."

"So, you go get checked out, make sure everything's all right." Earl sipped on his wine. "If it needs attention, you take care of it. Then get back in the game."

"If it's as bad as the doc said, that could take years."

"Screw the Stan. I have all the notes you e-mailed me. I'm sure you have more somewhere in a hard drive or something."

"About two terabytes worth of data."

"In a couple of weeks..." Earl turned to see if their wives were returning. They were, and Earl spoke faster. "I will set you up to see General Zeller. We'll go to the Pentagon, give him a debrief, some recommendations, then go from there."

"You're talking about *the* General Zeller?" Declan was always amazed at how deep Earl's contacts ran. "As in, US Army's head of intelligence? That Zeller?"

"Yeah, that General Zeller." Earl stood so that Vicki could take her seat.

After the bottle of fine wine was empty, Raf returned with another. Declan noticed the staff of servers standing by his side, holding enough plates of food to serve the entire Afghan Army. He couldn't stop thinking about Rex and the rest of the men over there, and he felt ashamed that he sat safely in Annapolis, ready to enjoy the town's best dining without his brothers-in-arms.

"One last toast before we start." Declan raised his glass. "To the men still fighting abroad."

"To the men," Earl repeated in a soft voice. "Now let's eat."

Declan reminded himself that he had everything he needed—his mentor, his woman, and an evening of celebration, however short-lived.

"Yes," he said, and squeezed Bran's hand. "Let's eat."

The evening finished after plenty of food, several bottles of wine, and endless joy. Earl and Vicki went back to their waterfront home while Bran and Declan returned to their cozy bed in the O'Callaghan.

He pulled her close to him, and she rested her hand against his face.

"They're great people," she said.

"And great parents," he told her. "Wait until you meet their kids. If anything, their lifestyle has strengthened their bonds."

"I hope that's the case with our children," she said.

"It will be." Lying on their sides, face-to-face on the bed, they gazed into each other's eyes.

"Dec," she said. "I'm pregnant."

At first unable to make sense of what she'd said, he shot up. "Oh, Bran, that's wonderful. Unbelievable." Then the fear crept in. "When did it happen?"

She giggled. "On that minibreak when you were on your way to Texas."

"But that was months ago."

"I know." A smile lit her face. "I'm in my second trimester, honey. The doctor's pretty sure that I'll go to full term this time."

THIRTY-THREE

B ran couldn't be happier. She snuggled beside him as he drove, her hand resting on his knee. The blue sky above was filled with cotton-ball clouds. They were finally headed home. Driving into the mountainous terrain of central Pennsylvania seemed to fill her with joy. He didn't want her to know that it made him think of eastern Afghanistan.

"Isn't it just beautiful?" She looked out the window and absorbed the view.

Declan didn't answer. He reached for the radio and turned up the volume. A classic rock station played *Squeeze Box* by the Who. It reminded him even more of Afghanistan.

"Honey, didn't you hear me?" Bran turned and looked at him. "I asked you a question."

"I'm sorry." He continued driving. "What did you ask?"

"Well, it was more of a comment." She turned down the radio. "I was just commenting on how gorgeous it is."

"Oh, yes. It's beautiful outside." He reached again for the volume knob, wondering whether every time the Who played on the radio he would have flashbacks of the day Samina was almost fatally shot. He wondered whether the day Haji Haq rescued him would forever be locked inside his mind. *Will my life be consumed with flashbacks?*

Bran grabbed his hand before he could turn up the song. "Is everything OK?"

Declan felt it was best to hide the truth. He had no reason to doubt Bran's understanding yet still felt the urge to keep everything inside. He feared she would ask too many questions.

"Absolutely. I still can't believe we're going to be parents."

"It looks that way. Last night was a perfect evening, and Vicki was really sweet." She grinned. "But I would have rather spent the night in bed with you."

"Me too. At least, now you know why I like those two so much."

"What are they, in their mid-fifties?" Bran asked. "It seems like they're inseparable. Totally in love."

"It's almost disgusting, isn't it?" He laughed. "But sometimes…"

"Sometimes, what?"

He didn't want to go on. *Sometimes great danger is the litmus test of love.*

"Sometimes I don't mind their lovey-dovey antics."

It wasn't what he meant to say, but it was close enough. She moved nearer and placed her head on his lap as he continued to drive to their quaint little farm home.

"I hope we'll be like that in thirty years, Dec."

"I'd bet on it."

Hours passed, and Bran fell asleep. He pulled up to their newly renovated home, and a wave of shock ran through his body. It was everything he'd hoped it would be.

"Wow." He put the car in park. "The house looks unbelievable."

"Wait till you see the inside." Bran wiped her eyes. "You're going to love it."

They had bags to carry in, but Declan didn't care. He jumped out and opened Bran's door. She reached for his hand, and the two of them ran toward the front door.

"I hear Apoc barking inside." Declan turned the handle. "You didn't leave him alone here, did you?"

"Of course not, silly. He stayed with my mom and dad." She leaned down to pet Apoc as he greeted them. "They brought him back here first thing this morning."

"Hey, buddy." Apoc covered Declan's face with sloppy kisses. "I missed you too."

"So what do you think?"

"Considering I just stepped foot inside and can only see the kitchen, its impressive. Really impressive."

"C'mon, I have a surprise for you." Bran ushered him to a nearby room. "This is your new office. I call it your Patriot Room."

The six-by-eight-foot room was completely renovated. The floor and ceiling trim was painted red, the wood around the windows was blue, and the walls were white. An old Civil War replica flag hung on one wall. Photos of Declan's previous military adventures and diplomas lined the walls along with photos of family members who once served in uniform. A small bookshelf and computer were perfectly positioned. The room was full but not cluttered.

"Bran, this is amazing," he said as his eyes began to water.

She rubbed his arm. "Let me show you the rest of the house."

Declan switched on the computer and allowed it time to boot. He hadn't heard from any of his buddies serving abroad in about a week. He desperately wanted to see if any e-mails had come through.

"No, sir. You're not working right now. You're coming with me so I can show you our new home."

"I'm right behind you," he said without protest.

Apoc wouldn't leave Declan's side. The house was perfect, and Declan felt at a loss for words. *Is this really where I belong?*

"Well?" Bran looked up at him. "Do you like it?

"Like it?" Declan picked her up by the waist and swung her around in a full circle. "I love it."

"I knew you would."

Declan walked outside and grabbed the bags they'd left in the car.

"Sweetie, I need to run out to the grocery store real quick." Bran realized that she forgot to stock the refrigerator before she went south. She wanted to cook a homemade dinner for Declan. "Do you need anything?"

"No. I'm fine." Once Declan had brought the bags inside, he immediately jumped on his computer.

With his e-mail open, he saw exactly what he was looking for, a note from Rex. After reading with great interest, Declan realized what time it was in Afghanistan. *Rex is awake. If he's on the FOB or at the Haj, he's probably on his computer right this minute.*

Declan clicked on his Skype icon. Rex was online. He clicked the call button. After several ringing tones, Rex answered.

"You made it back!" He could see Rex through the computer's live stream. "What took you so long?"

"Flew into BWI and stayed a couple of days." Declan was happy to see his brother in one piece, curly Viking hair wild as ever. "Went to Griff's funeral and wake, then linked up with my buddy and his wife in Annapolis."

"Earl?"

"Yeah." Declan wasn't allowed to tell anyone about Spartacus—but he'd mentioned his buddy Earl in Annapolis a few times.

"How's he doing?"

"You're at the Haj?" Declan ignored the question.

"Yeah, you left after we came back from what was probably the most FUBARed operation in Kunar, and I realized how screwed up things truly were." Rex pointed his computer behind him for a moment so Declan could see. "I brought some friends with me."

"Was that Jack and the guys?" Declan asked.

"Yup." Rex held up a bottle of rum. "They needed some R&R. You hear about Brett?"

"No. Is he OK?"

"He'll be fine. Messed up his knee pretty bad going down a mountainside on the Kunar mission." Rex hollered at the guys behind him to be quiet. "Doc Crooner did the same thing to him that he did to you. Sent him home."

"You got to be kidding me." Declan was amazed. "What a snake."

"Yeah, but the good news is, Brett should be on the East Coast in about a month. He said he was going to the left coast first, then was going to head over to Maryland to link up with some folks he knows. He was talking about building his own company."

"He mentioned something about starting a company when we were at Fort Hood."

"Well, it sounded like he was serious."

"Listen, Bran ran out to the store. She should be home any second now. I need to run. She wouldn't be happy seeing me on here within only a few hours of getting home. If you need anything, send me an e-mail. I'll try calling you in a couple days. I'll leave Skype on so you can call anytime."

"You got it, buddy. Tell your beautiful wife I'm still waiting for some photos of her single friends."

The call ended. Declan needed to channel all his thoughts and emotions before facing Bran. He missed Rex and the men tremendously. Deep down, he missed Afghanistan.

Being back in the States wasn't necessarily what he wanted, but being back with Bran was the one thing that could make up for leaving her alone. He loved her more than anything, and he could hardly wait to be a father. Yet he couldn't ignore the tug calling him back to his other life. Only time would tell how he would manage the transition. He hurried out to meet her as she pulled up with groceries, and made sure he was smiling as he did.

THIRTY-FOUR

A week passed, and Declan did his best transforming himself into a civilian and husband, into a normal, everyday guy. Yeah, that was him, all right. No one would have believed he had any other role, any other identity. Except Bran, maybe.

After several weeks of hiding both physical and mental pain, he knew it was time to see a neurosurgeon. It was the only way he could get back in country. Lacy Wong was respected by the guys he knew. She'd helped a lot of them, and he hoped that would be the case with him. Doc Crooner had to be wrong about his initial diagnosis. If a better one existed, Dr. Wong would find it.

"Mr. Collins, it's a pleasure meeting you." She was slender with jet-black hair pulled tightly into a bun, and everything about her and her office was professional. "Thank you for your service to our country."

Declan knew he was in good hands. "Well, Doc, I wish we didn't have to meet under these circumstances."

"It's unfortunate, of course." She smiled then took off her glasses, and placed them on her desk. "But it's also necessary. You know that."

"So when can I get back in the fight?" No use beating around the bush.

Dr. Wong pulled out Declan's recent MRI films and held them up to the ceiling light, taking one last look. He braced himself, knowing reality was about to hit.

"Declan, my husband went through trauma training. His roommate was a Navy SEAL. I know too well that guys like you have Type A personalities."

"Was never a SEAL, ma'am."

Her stern expression didn't falter. Declan realized as warm as she had initially appeared, she couldn't be won over. She was as direct as he was.

"Come." She reached for his hand, assisted him out of his chair, and pulled him toward her desk. Then she picked up a mock replica and handed it to him.

"This is a healthy spine of an adult male."

Declan held the plastic vertebrae as she went through every detail, from disks and nerves to the spinal sack and even the cord itself. He got a detailed lesson of the human neck in less than a minute.

"Mine looks just as good as this one, right?" He placed the replica back on the desk.

Dr. Wong shook her head almost apologetically. "Mr. Collins, I wish your spine looked this good."

"OK, so I'm a little banged up." Declan ran his fingers through his hair and tried to look calm. "Let's cut to the chase, Doc. Will you clear me to go back overseas?"

"Sit down." With an orange grease pencil in her hand, she began making circles on his MRI films. "Let me know when you want me to stop."

Declan's stomach began to turn. He knew the situation was worse than he could have expected and that nothing he said or did was going to change that. There was no escape. He had to take the news like a man.

"Your C-5, C-6, C-7, and C-8 are all compressed." She held the scan up to the light so Declan could see the newly drawn circles. "Your C-5 and C-6 are my biggest concern. You spinal sack is completely penetrated and is giving no protection to your spinal cord. I believe your cord is pinched behind your C-5. How you can actually walk is a miracle."

He remained silent, absorbing the news. Then he reached for the films she was holding to get a better look.

"Declan, I'm sorry, but as your doctor, I must tell you that in my honest, professional opinion, you will never go back into a war zone."

His eyes began to fill with tears. He blinked hard, but Dr. Wong didn't miss a thing. She sat next to him and placed her arm around his shoulder. Both of them sat silently for a moment.

Finally, Declan spoke. "OK, so I'm a bit broken. What do I need to do to make myself better? What types of exercises, what kind of stretching? Just tell me what I need to do."

"It's not that simple." Her voice had changed; it was much softer now. "You need surgery, a discectomy. It's the only way to fix this. I'm not saying you need it right away, but you will eventually. If you want, we can try everything in our power to help alleviate some of the discomfort, but in the end, you'll have to have surgery."

"And if I have this surgery, what are the odds that I'll be able to go back and serve abroad?" His gaze remained on his MRIs.

"Well, that depends on how well you heal, how well your body adapts, and how well your physical therapy goes."

He knew she was just trying to be positive. Her failure to look at him as she responded, and what she'd said earlier, was all the insight he needed. The visit was over.

"I'm afraid I have more disturbing news for you, Declan." Dr. Wong stood and looked down at him. "While I was outside looking at your films, my medical biller came to me and informed me that your insurance carrier is denying your claim."

"What?" He perched on the edge of the chair, confused. "What does that mean?"

"It means that they're not going to pay for any of your medical bills."

"How is that possible? They were the ones insuring me while I was overseas." His confusion turned to rage.

"Don't worry about this visit. It's on me. But you really need to get things worked out between you and your insurance carrier."

"This makes no sense." He began pacing the room. "How could they do this to me?"

"I suggest getting a really good attorney," she said. "Unfortunately, I've seen things like this happen before."

Declan tried to clear his head. There had been no letter in the mail from his insurance company, not even a phone call. They had totally bypassed him and gone directly to his neurosurgeon. He'd been betrayed.

After the visit, he darted to his truck. He grabbed his cell and called DC. He needed to contact his old employer.

"George," he told the receptionist who answered his call, "I need to speak with George Crawple. Let him know Declan Collins is on the line."

"I'm sorry, Mr. Collins. Mr. Crawple is on another call."

"Let him know that my insurance coverage was cancelled, and I need it activated ASAP." Sweat began to bead on his forehead.

"Mr. Collins, we cannot activate your insurance," she said. "Didn't you check the company e-mail?"

"Company e-mail? I haven't checked that in over eight months. We couldn't get online to the website due to Internet restrictions. You guys were supposed to use our DOD accounts for any e-mail."

"I'm sorry, Mr. Collins." She paused. "You have been terminated because you were kicked out of Afghanistan."

He felt as if she had slapped him. "I was not kicked out of Afghanistan," he said slowly. "I was told to come home to get medical treatment so that I would be allowed back in country."

"I'm sorry, sir."

"Sorry?" Declan was livid. "Sorry, my ass! I gave you all everything I had, and you're willing to take it away from me? Just like that?"

"Sir, I am only a secretary to Mr. Crawple. I am just letting you know why your coverage was canceled."

"Tell that son of a bitch he needs to call me ASAP."

The phone went silent. Declan sat in his truck in utter disbelief. How could any company be run like this? He was overwhelmed by anger and heartbreak.

Declan needed help. But where could he go? Who could he talk to? Bran would be home waiting for his return from the doctor's office. She wouldn't be prepared for the news.

Declan took a much longer route back to his house. He needed the extra time to hide his emotions. He didn't want to speak with Bran about his contract right away. The news about the surgery would be enough for one day. Perhaps with time and some answered prayers, he would get the wisdom needed to resolve the insurance issue before she caught wind.

THIRTY-FIVE

D eclan always sought an outlet for whatever was troubling him and today he found it outside in the crisp mountain air. Like a man on a mission, he cut firewood, mowed the lawn, and took care of the house. These tasks caused him physical pain but they were no match for his mental pain. Regardless of how hard he worked and how many times he reminded himself that he was home, Afghanistan and his brothers abroad never left his mind. No activity could take him far from the time he had spent in the Pashtun-dominated nation.

Haunted dreams began to disrupt his sleep. The nightmares became more and more frequent. Bran hadn't caught on yet, but she would soon if he didn't find some peace. The problem was, where to find it?

"I'm going to run to my classroom." Bran grabbed her car keys and gave him a kiss. "I want to make sure it's set up before the students come in next week. Are you OK?"

She was elegant in skinny jeans and a fringed black top that showed off her creamy complexion. A nasty voice in his brain demanded, *How can you leave her?*

"I'll be fine."

"You sure?"

Those eyes of hers probed, and he kissed her again to keep her from guessing the truth. "I need to do more work around here anyway."

"OK. I love you." The final kiss only stirred up more questions.

After she left, Declan wandered around the yard. He usually loved the end of August in this place. He welcomed the rush of fall. Today, though, he couldn't be distracted by the seasons. They would come and go, but he was frozen and removed.

He remembered something Rex had told him once as the two discussed faith. "As the saying goes, there are no atheists in foxholes."

Maybe that's what he needed. His faith had saved him before. Maybe it would save him again.

The church where he and Bran had married was only a few miles away, in the heart of town, and he decided to pay a visit. He found Father James tending the garden out front. He and Declan were far from soul mates, yet the elderly priest had seen combat. Maybe he would have some answers. Declan tried to catch his eye, but Father James was focused on the rose bushes.

Declan entered the church and stood in the doorway, staring at the brightly colored rays of sun shining through stained-glass windows. The church was empty. Good. In front of him rested an altar. Behind it, perched high above, hung a statue of Jesus nailed to a cross.

Here I am, Lord.

Declan walked forward, stopping himself at the wooden pew closest to the altar. He knelt, and did the sign of the cross to himself.

"Lord, you asked, 'and who shall I send?' Like Isaiah before me, when you asked, I volunteered. I placed my life on hold. I did it for you, Lord, for this nation, and for the future. You brought me home safely. You gave me strength, courage, and wisdom. But I feel torn. I need you now more than ever. I need that strength, courage, and wisdom now more than ever. Please, Lord, I need you." His emotions began to get the best of him.

His prayer brought him peace, yet his eyes became heavy with mist. The conflict in his head needed to be resolved.

After praying, he walked outside and saw that Father James was still gardening. Was it his imagination, or was the priest avoiding him?

There was only one way to find out.

"Hello, Father."

Father James looked up from his work, but he still held onto his pruning shears. "Declan. Welcome home. How are you doing?"

"It's hasn't been easy. I'm having a difficult time keeping things inside."

"You know, it won't get any easier if you hold everything in." Father James looked at him with soft, round blue eyes that looked much younger than his years. "You need to find a way to let things go, Declan. If you don't, you'll regret it later."

"I know. That's one reason I'm here this morning."

"What do you think you'll get from that?" The priest snickered out loud.

"Just looking for answers, Father." He hesitated. "My entire life, I did my best to maintain my faith. Now, I guess I'm just confused."

"That's understandable." He put down his pruning shears and took off his gardening gloves, but his expression was less than friendly. "Perhaps you're coming to understand why our church so vehemently opposes violence. You're having to live with the effects long after the battles are over."

He'd made a mistake trying to talk to this guy. To him, it was obvious that Father James had forgotten about Pope Urban II and the Crusades. "It's not over for me," Declan told him.

"I understand your frustration." The priest seemed to be speaking to a spot behind him. "I think it's time for you to take comfort in your faith."

"My faith is in God. That hasn't changed."

"Then God will give you comfort." The priest shifted where he stood. "Have you considered some medical help? I'd be happy to refer you to a professional in these matters."

Declan felt as if he'd been slapped. "And risk losing my security clearance? No way."

The priest narrowed his eyes. "Your job means more to you than your wellbeing? More than your relationship with your wife? More than the love of God?"

"My job has given me all of that—my wife and my relationship with God. That's why America is so beautiful. There are men, just as I am, who are willing to fight for our freedom. We are willing to sacrifice if we have to. I was at a military funeral recently…"

"The funeral of a friend?"

"More than a friend. A brother."

"Ah." The priest's eyes lit up. "Is that why you're struggling so hard right now?"

"No," Declan said. "I'm struggling because my brothers are still fighting, and I'm not. I feel like I've deserted them. *Never leave a brother behind*, we say, and that's what's tearing me apart right now."

"When I was in Nam, we left many behind, so I see your concerns." Father James nodded and gave Declan a self-satisfied smile. "I have to get going. I need to do my daily hospital run. I do have time for a confession, though."

There was time for a confession, but no time to talk. He was perplexed by the priest's attitude. Then again, Declan wasn't seeking some pity party.

"No need for that." He felt more lost than ever.

"If I recall, your last confession was at least six months ago." The blue eyes squinted in the sunlight.

"Eight months, Father. I was out fighting a war during those months."

"But of course. Even more reason for confession. I have the time."

"I don't." He said it before thinking.

"You obviously need some help."

That's what I've been trying to tell you. "Have a good day, Father." His throat tightened, and he could barely speak. "I need to get back home."

Declan questioned how any man could feel so empowered as a practitioner of faith yet be so fake when assisting the needy. Though Declan turned his back on Father James, he didn't turn his back on God.

THIRTY-SIX

D eclan hurried out the door in the early morning hours. Heavy fog engulfed the Pocono Mountains all around him. The rising sun penetrating the haze blinded his vision, but Declan was in the zone. He drove down I-95 to Washington. Earl had arranged a meeting with General Zeller at 1300. This was Declan's big chance to get back into the game.

Earl had supplied him with specific directions. Meet at the Ritz Carlton in Pentagon City at noon. Rehearse the brief with Earl. And then head over to the Pentagon at 12:30. The four-hour drive gave Declan plenty of time to run the meeting through his head. He believed he had nothing to worry about.

"Welcome to the Ritz Carlton, sir." The meticulously groomed parking valet in black pants and red jacket greeted Declan. "You'll be staying with us?"

"Just need it parked for a couple of hours." Declan discretely passed a fifty-dollar bill into the valet's hand.

"Enjoy your stay, sir." Parking valets were used to operators coming and going for short periods of time. Declan knew from experience: take care of valets, hotel managers, and bartenders. They're excellent lifelines.

Earl smiled as he entered the lobby.

"I take it you had no issues getting down here?"

"No, just blinded by the sun for about half the drive." Declan shook Earl's hand. "You ready to do this?"

"It's just another walk in the park." He led the way to the restaurant. There was no time to eat, so they ordered coffee.

"So, what's Zeller like?" Declan asked.

"He's a typical four-star. A politician." Earl threw the contents of a packet of synthetic sweetener into his cup. "He's not a friend, and don't forget that."

"So why the hell are we even speaking to him?"

"It's the game we have to play right now, Dec."

"Earl, Afghanistan isn't a game."

"Tactically, I couldn't agree with you more." He took a sip of his drink. "The general isn't a tactician, though. He's a strategist. And I believe you would agree that strategically, Afghanistan is a game."

"I get it."

"Do you?" Earl asked as he placed his cup on the table and stared into Declan's eyes. "Is what you and I are about to do truly clear to you? You have to be one hundred percent aware of what's going to happen."

"It's clear, Earl, crystal clear."

✝✝✝

Thousands of cars jammed the Pentagon parking lot and near the newly renovated bus station stood a swarm of office workers. Declan wasn't impressed by the security outside.

"This place is a suicide bomber's wet dream," he said.

"Come on. We have bigger fish to catch right now." Earl hurried past the rat race and entered the Defense Department's metropolis.

Major Kathy Lane greeted them at the visitor's check-in area. She was General Zeller's runner. A short, sharp, overly friendly woman, she radiated warmth. Declan liked her immediately.

"I don't know who you two are, but it's impressive getting a full hour with the general." Major Lane led the men past the Pentagon's internal mall and headed to Zeller's office situated on the second floor of the E ring, corridor four inside the Pentagon.

Earl glanced over at Declan and nudged his arm. "Major, we don't even know who we are these days. I guess that's what happens when you get to be my age."

"Actually, sir, you look familiar." The major turned and studied Earl's face. "Have you ever been on the news?"

"Yeah, he's a real celebrity." Declan laughed.

"Here we are, gentlemen." Major Lane opened the door to the office lobby. "Just have a seat, and I'll see if he's ready for you."

"Let him know that I don't have a lot of time to waste. I have to be on the news later today." Earl laughed at himself. "I'm just kidding, Major."

Declan was amazed. General Zeller had his own little army of workers answering phones, typing on computers, running fax machines. The outer office hummed with activity.

"All this for a four-star who's never seen combat a day in his entire career."

"Yeah, well, he obviously knew how to work the system," Earl replied in a low voice.

"Gentlemen, the general will see you now," said Major Lane.

Long ago, Earl had taught Declan about semiotics. What Declan observed didn't sit well with him. "He can't even get out of his office to greet us, what a pompous..."

"Behave," Earl ordered as they walked inside.

"Earl, it's nice seeing you again." General Zeller was a tall man, young for a four-star. "Declan, I've heard a lot of good things about you, son. Welcome home."

Declan wasn't happy being called *son* by the general, but he smiled anyway. "Thanks for taking the time to see us, sir."

"Have a seat." Zeller sat in his burgundy leather chair behind his mahogany desk. "So what can I do for you, gentlemen?"

"Mr. Collins just so happened to be in the area visiting, and I thought it would be a good idea for him to debrief you on the situation in Afghanistan." Earl was stretching the truth, of course. Declan wasn't just in the area visiting, and he was there for a purpose.

"Earl, don't you Agency folks realize that you're not the only ones with intelligence?" Zeller leaned forward and placed his elbows on the desk.

"Funny, sir, but you're more than well aware that I retired several years ago."

Zeller turned his gaze on Declan. "Son, do you really believe you're going to tell me something about Afghanistan that I don't already know?"

"General, I don't know everything about Afghanistan." Declan sat up straighter in the chair. "But I do have insight that even Big Army doesn't possess."

"Really?" General Zeller didn't even try to hide his narcissism. "Well, you tell me one thing about Afghanistan you think I don't already know, and I'll determine whether to continue this conversation."

The spotlight was on Declan. He wondered if this meeting would have gone better without Earl being present. It was obvious Zeller didn't take too kindly to Agency folks.

"Fifty former Muj leaders are rotting away in eastern Afghanistan," Declan said. "They have access to thousands of fighters willing to take on the Taliban. They are waiting for us to give them the green light."

"That's what you're here to tell me?" Zeller stretched back in the chair. "So you want me to arm a bunch of local Afghan fighters so they can later use those weapons against my troops?"

"Sir, the leader of the bunch is a feared man, an honest man. Sure, he doesn't care too much for the United States because we screwed his people after the Russians left, but he hates the Taliban even more."

"Son, you swallowed too much of that Pashtun Kool-Aid."

"The guy's name is Mehsud Haq," Declan said, and forced himself to keep his cool. "He saved my life. Sacrificed his own son so I along with a team of OGA could live. It's not Kool-Aid, sir. It's reality."

"The Afghan's time is up," Zeller said. "We're going to begin negotiating with the Taliban here real soon."

"Negotiate?" Earl was livid, his face red beneath his white hair.

"General," Declan said. "If the United States negotiates with the Taliban, we'll be responsible for a complex genocide. Every Afghan military, police, border guard—anyone who ever worked with the coalition will be killed on the spot."

"Well, I wish you would have told me this insight about the Muj about three years ago." General Zeller didn't intend to budge.

"The war was won in '02 by our SF. They used many Muj factions, and they weren't all just Northern Alliance," Earl chimed in.

"You would have known this long ago if you would have just watched and observed. Declan just confirmed that what happened in '02 could happen today, General. There's still time to create an exit plan that will allow our troops to come home with their heads held high."

"Sorry, gentlemen. The SECDEF and POTUS want to negotiate." Zeller stood to walk them out.

"General," Declan said at the door. "One last thing, if I may."

"What is it, Declan?" Earl asked, his expression a combination of warning and confusion.

General Zeller seemed just as surprised that Declan hadn't taken the hint: the meeting had been adjourned. "Yeah, what now?"

"I know you have a bunch of chatter presenting a million different leads as to where your number one high-value target is." Declan turned to Earl. His eyes told his mentor to brace himself for what was to come.

"Well, of course we have chatter." Zeller's laugh was forced.

"You want Zawahiri?" Declan asked. "He travels from Pakistan into Kunar. His entry points vary, but he always goes into the Nari, Dangam, and Sirkanay districts. He only uses Sirkanay when he wants to go into Nangahar Province, which is rare. More often, he goes into Dangam. He only goes into Nari when he wants to go into Nuristan."

"Interesting. But, son, we already did Operation Red Wing hunting Bin Laden in Kunar. That turned into a nightmare before we finally got him in Abottabad."

"Sir, you've known that he goes into Kunar. Well, now you know his rat lines."

"Not enough insight, no vetting. This means nothing to me."

"Show him your thumb drive," Earl said.

With Keller's nod, Declan placed his thumb drive into the

general's computer. He opened a file of photos, which showed positive identification for well over fifteen high-value targets. Each man's face was clearly recognizable, and each man's name was under his photo.

"Where did you get these from?" the general demanded.

"One of my sources in country is an actual Taliban Commander. He's in a power struggle and willing to flip on every one of these targets. We have an opportunity here through him and through my Muj contacts to start a civil war among the different enemy factions. I provided him with a unique camera, and he took the photos for me. It's a camera that no one in Afghanistan can get their hands on, proving that I provided it. Now, is this vetted enough?"

General Zeller's ears were red. "Go back to Zawahiri."

"I told you his entry points," Declan said. "There are three of them. He only has two staging locations inside Pakistan." He took out the thumb drive.

"Go on."

"Bin Laden hung out in Khushab and Abbottabad, Pakistan. Well, those two locations are also where Zawahiri hangs around. More today in Khushab because of the successful OBL operation." Declan handed his thumb drive to Earl for safekeeping. "Abbottabad is home to one of Pakistan's largest military training facilities. No one would have ever thought OBL would have made the place his home. Well, no one has been thinking about Khushab, one of Pakistan's most secured weapon facilities, either."

"OK, this is getting more and more outlandish." General Zeller again headed for the door. "Thank you, men, for stopping by. Welcome home, Declan."

Earl gently eased Declan out the door.

Major Lane walked the two out of the Pentagon. Declan was

speechless. Earl embraced small talk with the Major as if the meeting had never happened.

"You did exactly what I needed you to do," Earl said as he opened his car door. "You were spot on."

"I felt like killing his condescending ass." Declan entered the passenger side.

"You held in your frustration well." Earl drove back to the Ritz. "You showed him that you're the real deal. You left him thinking."

"Thinking?" Declan asked. "No, that jerk is sitting back in his desk with his feet up probably laughing hysterically at us right now."

"No, he's thinking really hard." Earl pulled up to the Ritz. "Listen to me. You did exactly what I needed you to do today. You may not understand now, but tonight you will."

"Tonight?"

"Yeah, we're going to dinner. I arranged for a few of my buddies to get together and have dinner at Carpino's."

Declan's phone rang. "It's Brett. I told you about him already, right?"

"Former Delta guy?"

"Yeah that's him, I think he's in Baltimore right now. Let me answer this." Declan took the call.

"Hey, Brother," Brett said. "I'm in Baltimore. Got some great news."

"Have him meet us tonight," Earl whispered.

"Brett, I'm in a meeting right now down in DC. Can you meet for dinner tonight in Annapolis? A place called Carpino's."

"Absolutely, what time?"

"I'll text you the details." Declan rushed the conversation. "Give me about an hour, and I'll let you know. I need to run."

"You got it." Brett ended the call.

Earl seemed pleased. Declan didn't understand why he wanted Brett present tonight, but he was smart enough to simply sit back and learn. The master was working, and Declan knew he was a major part of the master's plan.

"Follow me to my house." Earl leaned over as Declan got out of the car. "I'll see you when we get back to my house. I'll fill you in then."

Declan was still confused, but he maintained his poise. "You got it, boss. I'll see you then."

Declan jumped in his pickup and realized he'd told Bran that he would be home tonight. How would she react to his staying a day longer than expected? Declan hoped that she would be understanding. After all, he would be in good hands with Vicki and Earl. Earl didn't play games. If he needed him to stick around, it was the right thing to do.

THIRTY-SEVEN

As they pulled up to Earl's mini-mansion, Declan realized he was still steamed. The general didn't want to learn from him. He just wanted to be right. But Earl said the meeting was a tactical success, and he had to believe him.

"Call Brett. Just have him meet us here," Earl said once they were standing on the circular drive in front of his home. "We can all head to Carpino's together."

Declan did as he was told. Brett agreed to the rendezvous and said he would be at Earl's in thirty minutes.

"Come in," Earl said. "Want a drink?"

"I'm good." Declan took off his shoes and entered the large cherry-wood hall. "So, what's going on?"

"Still thinking about Zeller?" Earl asked.

"Not necessarily Zeller. Rather the day as it unfolds." Declan looked out the kitchen door overseeing the pool. "I'm a little lost here, Earl."

"I've always taken care of you." He slid open the door and walked out near the pool. "Let me ask you something."

"Shoot."

"I've never met anyone who has so many tactical guys at his disposal. You just asked some guy who never met me, has no clue who I am, to come over to my house. Your guys love you." Earl sat on a canvas recliner. "I have all the strategic folks at my disposal. Former generals, SECDEFs, politicians, business owners, and even media. The two of us have the ultimate system. We can do things no one could ever imagine."

"So what's your question?" Declan asked and sat next to him.

"Do I really need to ask?"

"No."

Declan knew that Earl was building the ultimate network of operators. With these operators, he could make things happen no one else could. He could obtain funds, align with national security objectives, and secure America.

Just then, Brett drove up to the driveway. Earl's two guard dogs barked, sounding the alarm of his arrival.

"He's here." Declan jumped out of his seat. "He mentioned that he had some good news. It'll be interesting to hear what he has to say."

Brett was dressed in jeans, a white button-down, and a blazer. Declan almost didn't recognize him without his beard.

"Hey, Brother." Brett rushed through the doorway and gave Declan a hug. "Still won't shave that thing?"

"Thought I was going back, but it seems God has other plans for me." Declan was happy to see a fellow warrior. "Brett, this is Earl."

"Heard a lot of good things about you." Earl led the way inside. "Can I get you something to drink?"

"Just some water, please."

"So what's all this jibber about you having some good news?" Declan asked.

"Is this photo real?" Brett had snooped around the living room and spotted a picture of Earl with former president George W. Bush. "My apologies, Earl, but I didn't know you had so many contacts in such high places."

"See the one with Rummy?" Earl handed Brett a glass of water and showed him a photo of former secretary of defense Rumsfeld and him together. "He's a true super patriot, a great man. Both of them are."

"You know, a lot of my former classmates would disagree with you." Brett turned and continued to look around the living room. "They would say the two were war mongers."

"Is that how you feel?" Earl asked.

"I don't know if I told you this," Declan said. "But not only was Brett here in Delta, he also got his master's from Harvard."

"Harvard? You got to be kidding me." Earl laughed. "In what field?"

"Business." Brett glanced out the backyard then over to Declan. "That's the good news, Dec."

"What?"

"I just met with some old friends of mine. We decided to start our own company." Brett followed Declan outside and took the lawn chair Earl pulled out for him.

"What type of company?"

"Defense contracting," Brett said. "Train, mentor, and advise. A lot of intel work."

"I love it," Earl said. "This is great news."

"Dec, you heard that, because you and I were removed from Afghanistan, neither of us is on the contract anymore, right? You did get the e-mail?"

"I haven't been able to check e-mail in a couple days," he said, stunned. "So were we fired?"

"Pretty much."

"Those assholes!" Declan threw himself back in the chair. "They better take care of my medical bills."

"I highly doubt it. Before I came to Baltimore, I tried using the insurance they provided and was declined." Brett stood and walked closer to the pool. "If I were you, I'd find me one hell of an attorney."

"The same happened to me..." Declan felt as if he'd been shot in the chest. The day had not gone as planned, and Brett's news had just made it worse. Not only had he been denied health coverage, but now he was being cut loose completely.

This time, the news came as less of a surprise. It was as if he'd hardened since the visit to Dr. Wong, and the sense of betrayal began to dissipate from his chest sooner. Luckily, Bran had medical insurance through her job, and he could be placed on it too.

"So what's this dinner all about?" Brett walked back over to where Declan and Earl were seated.

"I'm about to make your company grow into something you could never have imagined." Earl snickered.

"How do you mean?" Brett sat back down.

"He meant to say, *we're* going to make your company grow into something you could never have imagined." Declan smiled at Earl, reassuring his mentor that he was onboard. And he was. Now more than ever.

THIRTY-EIGHT

Declan's emotions were conflicted, trapped in his head. Regardless of how hard he tried, he couldn't get them out.

He was going to be a dad.

He was never going to be able to go back overseas.

He'd been betrayed by the very government he had believed in. The private contractor he worked for was one hundred percent funded by the government. Due to Department of Labor laws through the Defense Base Act and the War Hazards Act, the government protects contract companies but does nothing to protect the contracted—America's secret warriors.

Yet his work didn't feel finished. There had to be something left for him, something new.

When he was in the Stan, no sacrifice would have been too great for him. He could have ended up like Brett, losing his family. He could have ended up like Griff, losing his life. Yet when he had needed support from his government, he had realized he was standing alone. No, not alone. Earl had never turned his back on him, and right now, Declan knew that thanks to Earl's belief in him, his journey would be taking a new direction.

He had followed Earl's lead and was wearing a black suit with no tie and black cowboy boots. Brett was beside him. Declan could see he was determined to conceal the pain his divorce was causing him. His well-pressed gray suit looked new, and he'd cut and gelled his spiky red hair.

"You OK?" Declan asked.

"Still trying to figure out what I'm doing here," he said.

"Trust Earl," he told him. "I do."

Brett gestured to the crowd. "How are we going to have any privacy?"

"Good question."

He had realized Carpino's would be packed, but not this packed. he hadn't accounted for the families of the Annapolis students returning from summer break. Even Raf appeared to be overwhelmed as he greeted Earl and the rest of them at the door as he always did.

The men they were going to meet were what Earl always called "the brains." They were the strategic planners, a secret society whose existence was unknown even to the government.

Earl appeared calm and unruffled by the noise and activity around them.

"Guys," he said, "do me a favor and order me a water from the bar."

Then he headed toward the back of the restaurant, where Raf was assisting some of his wait staff.

"Can I get one water and a Yuengling?" Brett waved down the bartender. "What can I get you, Dec?"

"I think I'm good for now." He scanned the restaurant. "Don't know how long we'll be here. Surprised it's this busy. It's not the kind of environment I imagine Earl would want for this kind of thing."

"What do you mean? We're just having dinner, right?" Brett tipped the bartender.

"Nothing Earl does is what it appears. Everything has an agenda."

Earl headed back toward the bar. Declan noticed his shit-eating grin and knew that something had happened. Or was about to.

"So, what's going on?" he asked.

"Nothing. We're just fine."

"I need a minute." Declan picked up Earl's goblet of ice water and handed to him. "Got to call Bran and let her know I won't be home tonight."

Without waiting to discuss it, he walked outside. The street in downtown Annapolis was busy. Midshipmen trickled back toward the academy, and their parents walked with them, talking quietly, arms around each other. Declan loved knowing those kids would lead tomorrow's Navy.

Bran wasn't home. He left a message. "Love you, honey. I'm with Earl at a meeting, and I'll be staying with him and Vicki. Everything's fine. See you tomorrow."

Meanwhile, he kept his eyes on his surroundings. Walking in his direction, a familiar figure appeared. It was Charles Becker, the suit.

"Charles." Declan extended his hand. "How are you?"

"Mr. Collins, nice to see you made it." His dark gray Van Dyke beard looked painted on. It contrasted his brown hair and made him appear even more distinguished.

"I sent you an e-mail." Declan shook his hand. "Never heard back from you."

"What do you mean?" Charles patted him on the shoulder. "I'm here now."

It was obvious to him that Earl had invited Charles to dinner. Who the other guests would be remained a mystery.

"Do you know who else is coming?"

"Big dogs," Charles replied. "One of them was my colleague at

INSCOM."

Big dogs for sure. Declan knew all about the Information and Security Command.

"That must have been one crazy assignment."

"Not nearly as crazy as my time running MACV operations in Nam." The suit grinned. "Let's go inside and get a drink."

Earl met his eyes as they walked in. "Charles," he said. "It's great seeing you again. I see you met my friend Declan Collins. Let me introduce you to one of his counterparts. He used to run ops with him in Afghanistan, Brett Walker."

"Mr. Becker, it's nice meeting you." As Brett turned to face him his eyes widened. "Actually, we met a couple of times. I did some debriefs for you many years ago."

"Yes, I remember. It was Captain Walker back then, wasn't it?"

"A couple more are coming," Earl told them. "We can wait here by the bar and have some drinks, or we can go to our table now."

Everyone agreed to wait by the bar. Declan felt out of place. He never was in Special Forces, and he never held any prestigious positions; he had never been a clandestine operator from the CIA or an Under SECDEF. He knew better than to allow anyone to observe his discomfort.

From a distance, he noticed the restaurant manager.

"Earl, Raf is headed our way."

"Excellent. This is our night, Dec. I hope you're ready."

"Let's make this happen." Declan walked toward Raf and waved the group to head in his direction.

"It's time to build the mother ship," Earl whispered. "The ultimate system."

Raf ushered the four of them to a room tucked away from the rest of the patrons. Immediately, Declan noticed there was only one way in and one way out. After spending time in the Stan, he wasn't all that keen on single-entry points, but this would have to do.

A few minutes passed, and as they sat at their hideaway dinner table, three more men entered the room. One shouldered a soft black case, which Declan knew held some type of weapon.

Earl continued with more introductions. The group included a former Air Force deputy chief of staff lieutenant general, a weapons manufacturer, and an active CIA operator. Finally, after the fiasco with General Zeller earlier in the day, Declan felt at ease. He was surrounded by some of the brightest and most patriotic men in the country.

"Gents," Earl said. "Now that we are all acquainted, let's take our seats, have some drinks, feast on some good chow, and discuss our future." He took a seat across from Declan on the side of the table. "Charles, why don't you sit at the head?"

"Thanks, Earl." The suit took his seat. "Looking around the room, it is obvious to me why Earl wanted us all to get together. First, let me say thanks to him for making this happen. Second, I believe it's paramount that we discuss our nation's future. Everyone, look around this room. Look at the caliber of men we have sitting here. In all my years serving this nation, I have never been in a room with such amazing patriots."

"Here, here," Earl barked. "If you guys could have been flies on a wall earlier this afternoon and seen my young protégé in action against General Zeller, you would have fallen out of your chairs. Never in my life have I exited a general's office with him thinking the way Declan here made him do."

"What was that conversation about?" the suit asked.

"That's not important right now," Earl replied. "What's important is that with us tonight we have two young men whose careers are about to be crushed if we don't come together."

"What do you mean?" the suit asked.

"What he means, sir, is both Brett and I have been taken out of the system as military advisors." Declan paused. "Someone at the top wants us out. For us, and excuse me, Brett, if I'm out of line speaking for you here, this war isn't over."

"That's correct." Brett said. "Guys like us are being shafted all the time. This is why I, along with hundreds of guys like me, are starting our own companies."

"Afghanistan is just a little fiasco the United States sucked itself into," the suit said. "This line of business is all about saving our nation and making money at the same time. I'm sure others around the table can identify about a dozen small countries we can manipulate right now."

"Virtually any country in South America, Africa, and Southeast Asia are hot for the Agency," Earl chimed in. "Our HUMINT capabilities are limited in those regions. We have to outsource most of that."

Declan realized where all of this was going. "So with the proper contacts, the right sources and assets, we can make things happen without setting foot where DOD or the State Department has a large presence. Right?"

"Exactly. The key to making money, and I mean real money these days, isn't through contracting yourself out to the US government." The suit sipped on his wine. "You want to protect the United States yet make real money—that doesn't come in any US currency."

"Natural resources?" Declan asked.

"Exactly," Earl continued. "Oil, cocoa, minerals, diamonds, whatever. If it's a commodity, operate through tradeoffs."

"Seems complex," Brett said. "How do you get those items into the United States? How do you refine them to make them worth anything?"

"With the right people working alongside you, anything is doable," Earl replied. "This is how I used to do things when I worked for the Agency. We never did anything with cash."

Lightbulbs flashed on inside Declan's head. Earl was a genius. Still, he was concerned this could turn into a war-profiteering initiative.

"Let me get this straight," he said. "We identify world-wide hotspots, places of concern for national security. We go in, work a deal to let's just say, train, mentor, and advise, then get paid in goods?"

"That's where Brett's bank of operators comes in," Earl said.

"Yes, but it's deeper than that." The suit reached down and lifted the soft black case from beside his CIA counterpart. "We also sell military equipment." With that, he pulled out a brand new military-grade assault weapon from the case and laid it on the table.

"Holy shit." Brett's eyes grew large.

"That's where the real money comes in." Earl raised his voice. "We won't need to worry about ITARS compliance either. I'll have that taken care of."

"I never thought about the International Traffic in Arms Regulations," Declan revealed. "That's a tough one, but if anyone can deal with ITARS compliance, it's those sitting in this room right now. Everything's one hundred percent legal?"

"It has to be." Earl swallowed his water. "Everything must be done by the book. Anyone crosses the line, well, I won't go there."

A knock sounded on the door and the suit quickly put the gun back in its case. Servers carried steaming platters in. Business was done. A feast was before them, and Declan's head was spinning.

When the wait staff left, Earl asked, "Who's in?"

Everyone nodded. There were no questions. The most powerful system next to that of America's founding fathers had just been brought to life.

Declan realized that by being in the same room with these men, he was back in the game. He finally felt alive again. For him, this war hadn't ended. Oh, no. It had just begun.

Acknowledgments

After serving the United States for as long as I have, it's impossible to thank everyone who played a significant part in my life. I won't even make the attempt. But of course, I would be a fool not to thank my entire family for always being by my side, especially my wife. Without all of you, friends included, I wouldn't be the man I am today.

I'm not one to look for any cool points, and many readers may dislike what I am about to say. I am not a Holy Roller by any stretch of the imagination but I do believe in God. I've seen and done things I wish I never had to see and do. I am confident God exists because while facing many austere predicaments, I have felt my feet be lifted off the ground by a magical force, which brought me to a safer place. Thanks, God, for looking out for me. I live because of you.

Though this book is a novel, it could be construed as historical fiction. I'm not one for labels. I leave it up to the reader to decide which label describes this book for them. I will tell you flat out, though, that this book was inspired by some very real people and some very real events.

Yes, there is a real Rex Bowbart, Spartacus, Baba Rich, etc.— names were changed to protect their identities. Every one of them is a hero to me. I know what they have done for the United States and I know what they continue to do. I could never thank them enough for what they have done, not just for me, but for the United States of America.

236

Most importantly, I would like to thank those who gave up everything for this great nation. Specifically, I would like to thank America's secret warriors—contractors. The work they do day in and day out will never receive the praise it deserves.

Many contractors are no longer with us. Families will continuously grieve the loss of sons, daughters, mothers, fathers, etc. But like our military members who have fallen before us, contractors too shall never be forgotten.

MSGT (Ret.) Robert Pittman, a former Fifth Group Special Forces member, quickly turned contractor after retiring from the US Army. He was killed in Afghanistan on July 29, 2010. I never had the privilege or honor to work alongside Robert but I feel like I have known him for a very long time.

Robert's mother, Vicki Pittman, was the first person to contact me after a Fox News article I had written about US defense contractors. She thanked me for praising their courage, honor, and love for this great country.

Vicki and I have stayed in contact ever since. Thanks to the virtual world, I feel like she and I have created an unbreakable bond. She has become a mother figure for me. Not a mother through blood, but a mother for respecting the work her son Robert and I have fulfilled. I cannot thank Vicki enough for all the strength, courage, and wisdom she has shared with me over the past couple of years.

Lastly, I would like to thank all the folks at Quiet Owl Books for helping me publish this story. You're magically talented people. Thank you.

To Be Continued...

W hat do warriors do when wars end? For some, wars never end. During a time when rogue regimes rely upon proxy, incorporating terrorism into their arsenals, and threatening the safety of the United States, super patriots come together, willingly risking everything to secure a nation.

Book two, *Contracted: America's Terror Trackers*, is a novel inspired by real people and real events. It takes the reader deep into the underground world of clandestine operations involving America's fiercest operatives.

Sign up to stay updated at
Kerry-Patton.com

Please honor those who have served.
Kerry-Patton.com

Made in the USA
San Bernardino, CA
08 August 2013